THE BRIDAL SHOP

THE ROSE SISTERS, BOOK 1

SIENNA CARR

CHAPTER 1

.

"You look absolutely stunning," said Ashleigh. She watched as friends and family of the bride gasped, their hands clutching their chests as they looked at the bride in the wedding dress she had just put on. This was the last fitting, and everyone was in awe. Tears threatened to fall from many eyes. Murmurs of approval mingled with long sighs, creating a chorus of wonderment. The bride-to-be's mother looked joyous. "My baby girl," she cried.

"Mom!" Helena, the happy bride-to-be and, even more importantly for the Rose sisters, an extremely satisfied customer, fanned her face and at the same time admired her reflection in the large ornate mirror.

"I *love* this." She smoothed down the rich satin of her dress then adjusted her veil, turning to look at herself from all angles. Her friends and family took pictures on their cell phones.

"Oh, my word." Eloise, Ashleigh's sister and co-owner of The Bridal Shop, along with their youngest sister, Ginny, dutifully sighed and gushed. This had been months in the making; not the dress, it wasn't made by them, but the entire operation from consultations to helping the bride find her perfect dream dress, and making alterations and so forth, took a while.

Ashleigh and her sisters were less in the business of selling dresses and more in the business of selling dreams. The Bridal Shop sold ready-to-wear bridal dresses made by a variety of manufacturers and designers, and with Eloise's artistic flair and eye for fashion, they could find the dream dress that would make a bride look perfect on her big day.

The dress was indeed beautiful.

"You'll look stunning walking down the aisle," Ashleigh told her. She had watched this exact same scenario play out many times over the twenty-plus years of running the family's business. She had seen thousands of happy brides start their journeys here, and it always began with the dress.

"Where dreams begin," someone in the bride's party said. "It's true, it's so true."

"Yes, they do ..." the new bride-to-be echoed. "Where dreams begin, they do begin here, and *now* ..." The smile on her face spread out as she repeated the slogan which was synonymous with The Bridal Shop, the business Ashleigh and her sisters all worked at, the one her parents set up so long ago.

Where dreams begin.

The words were written in cursive gold writing on a cream silk painted wall, and it caught people's attention as soon as they walked in, putting them in the right state of mind for fulfilling their dreams.

Unfortunately, those words didn't have the same effect on Ashleigh and she forced herself to smile and nod in agreement.

Her dreams hadn't begun here. They had died.

"It fits perfectly," said Eloise, fussing around the bride. Of the three of them, Eloise was the one who had studied fashion and design and was the better equipped to deal with the actual design and fitting side of things. The business had been started by their mother many years ago. She had been the real figurehead behind the company.

"I'll leave you to it." Ashleigh left the enraptured group and walked over to the counter in order to get away. Sometimes, happy brides were more than she could handle.

She waited patiently by the counter, then checked the appointment book to see if there were any more fittings for dresses later today.

"I love your shop." A woman, probably an elderly aunt, walked over to her. "It has such a lovely feel to it. We knew it was something special the moment we walked in."

"Thank you. That's exactly the feeling we want you to have," Ashleigh replied. Customer feedback, and compliments especially, told her that they were doing things right. Over the years, she and her sisters had strived to make The Bridal Shop the number one wedding dress shop in Whisper Falls and the surrounding areas.

"Not to mention that your dresses are amazing, so beautiful, such a selection and the service you ladies provide is out of this world. I will definitely be recommending you."

"Thank you."

"How long have the three of you been running this business?"

"Twenty-two years," Ashleigh replied, forcing a smile she didn't feel. Once upon a time, it had been true. She had loved it here, running and growing the business that her beloved parents had started, until the fatal car accident had shattered their lives. The shock of losing both parents, so young and so unexpectedly, had blindsided them.

Ginny had been a mere toddler. "An accident," her mother had said, when a third child had been born so many years later. "A *happy* accident." The eighteen-year age gap between Ashleigh and her youngest sister sometimes made their relationship seem more like that of a mother and daughter, than that of sisters.

"Twenty-two years! You don't look old enough to be running something for that long." The usual surprise followed. Ashleigh didn't look her forty-three years. She was still on the tall side, and slim and svelte, though maybe not having had any children was the reason why. All three sisters were tall but Ginny was voluptuous and more rounded. Eloise was the tallest of them all, with long arms and legs. The Rose sisters didn't look like sisters at first glance, save for her and Ginny who shared their mother's hair color, although Ashleigh had hazel eyes. Eloise's dark brown hair and eyes were similar to their father's.

Twenty-two years she had stayed, running a business she'd never had any plans to run, and living in a small town she had wanted to leave so long ago. And here she was. Stuck.

"Where dreams begin, I love that," said another member of their entourage.

"Thank you." Ashleigh had to bite her tongue. For twenty-two years, she had stared at those words knowing that they weren't true. Not for her.

But in the beginning, the grief of losing both parents had been a shock that had devastated all of their young lives. And over the years, especially during the last three, a simmering resentment had started to creep up inside her each time she walked into the shop and saw those words. It had gotten to the point that she found herself staring at the slogan with the stark realization that her dreams had ended the day her parents had died.

Her mother had been smart, and astute, and Ashleigh missed her sorely. Her heart had been shredded to lose her parents, but the loss of her mother—her mentor, guide and friend—that loss had ruptured and caused a gaping hole in her young life. She knew it was one she would never get over.

How different all of their lives would have been had that truck not jack-knifed across the highway, causing fatal collisions and a pileup of the cars behind it.

The sisters had changed things at The Bridal Shop in recent years, moving away from their original location on Main Street to bigger premises slightly away from the busy town center. Moving to a more picturesque building surrounded by trees and greenery had worked out so well. They had changed the look and feel of the shop, making it more upscale, so that it seemed more like a high-end boutique than just a regular store. The addition of red velvet chaise lounges and chandeliers had transformed The Bridal Shop into a place that many from out of town came to visit. Some of the dresses they sold were sourced from new and upcoming designers. In this way, they were positioned perfectly for customers who wanted 'exquisite' without the Rodeo Drive prices. Because of their special relationship with the designers and manufacturers, they were able to also provide tailor-made dresses at a higher price for the more discerning clients, like Ginny. As a co-owner, she got such perks.

Many customers, though, were happy with the choice of ready-to-wear dresses they stocked. Many customers visibly gasped when they entered and saw the mannequins dressed in organza tulles and silk and satin dresses in white, cream or ivory.

"Dreams really do begin here, don't they?" the woman continued, obviously eager to chat. "It's the absolute truth, a woman wears this dress for one day, and takes her vows and makes a commitment, and then she starts a new life."

Ashleigh held her smile.

"How long have you been married?" the woman asked her. Ashleigh always found it odd how people presumed that she was married, despite her not wearing a wedding ring.

"I'm not married."

The woman's' face dropped. "Oh, I ... I ... I assumed."

"People often do."

"You've never married?" The woman stared at her as if she'd caught the plague.

"Mom! Stop being so nosy," a young woman hissed before giving Ashleigh an apologetic look.

"It's fine. I get asked this a lot." People assumed these things. She had never married, though Eloise had tried it, for about eleven months, before that ended. "But Ginny's getting married." She nodded towards her sister. "Next month."

A chorus of approval and excitement rose up. "How lovely!"

"Your dress must be amazing," the younger girl exclaimed to Ginny.

"Oh, it is. It's beautiful," Ginny gushed.

Ashleigh let out a small breath. "Only the best for this one," she muttered to herself. Ginny's dress had taken twice as long to finalize as most. She kept changing her mind, for one thing, and always wanting something else the moment she saw the new designs from their suppliers. Finding the perfect wedding dress for Miss Genevieve had been a continuously moving goal.

But now, it was done. Ginny's dress was ready, and with a month to go before her big day, Ashleigh was biding her time before making her announcement. Or, perhaps, she would do it before then.

"I want to get my dress from here, Mom." Ashleigh surveyed the young woman and recalled being that age. Her own dreams hadn't had a chance to start. She'd given it all up, the plans to travel for six months before leaving to go to Boston where Ford, the love of her life, would start working at his uncle's firm and she would start a degree in journalism.

That had been the plan, until life happened and changed everything. She had abandoned those plans and done the right thing. She had stayed behind to take care of the business her parents had built up, and to keep the family together. With the help of Aunt Becky, her mom's older sister, who also never married or had children, she had kept her siblings together and done her best to maintain some semblance of family life, even though the people who had given her life were no more.

Watching everyone else's dreams begin while hers had stagnated was becoming harder to swallow.

It was time to change things. To fix things. To put things right. She was patiently waiting for Ginny's wedding to be over with and then she would make her announcement, because soon it would be time for *her* dreams to begin.

CHAPTER 2

"*I* liked her buttons. My dress would look better with the satin buttons, like Helena had, don't you think?" Ginny rifled through the wedding dresses hanging on the clothes rail.

Eloise slapped her hand playfully. "She's taken her dress. It's not here."

"But there was another one with satin buttons. I saw it a few days ago."

"Will you stop putting your hands over these, Ginny?" Eloise looked displeased. She was particularly protective about the dresses. She and a few of the part-time assistants did the alterations as and when needed. Ginny handled the marketing and Ashleigh took care of the bookkeeping; these were the primary duties assigned to each of them though together they handled whatever needed to be done in the business. There was a schedule in place, and they took turns working on Saturday and having one day off in the week to make up for it.

"My hands are clean and I was only taking a look." Ginny stood back, hands on hips, defiant.

"What is it with you and everyone else's dresses? Your dress is gorgeous, and you should be happy with it," Eloise countered.

"I *am* happy with it, but we own a bridal dress store and you can't blame me if I get new ideas and want changes."

"Get new ideas and want changes?" Eloise cried. "You always want changes."

"How can I not when I'm surrounded by so many gorgeous dresses!" Ginny's eyes flashed.

"Your dress is being delivered next week. I am not asking for any more changes to be made, not even the buttons! We already changed them from lace to silk."

Ashleigh listened to the verbal sparring between her sisters and held her tongue. Ginny was never satisfied and she always had her eyes on all the wedding dresses. It didn't help that they owned a bridal shop. It also didn't help that she and Eloise spoiled her. She had been almost three years old when they'd lost their parents, and Aunt Becky had stepped in as their guardian even though Ashleigh had been of age to take care of her siblings. Ginny had been too young to remember that time as painfully as she and Eloise did.

"What do you want to change now?" Ashleigh asked, her patience beginning to wear thin as she tapped the keys on her cell phone harder than she intended. She was going to slip away and disappear into the office sometime soon, before she gave in and let Ginny have her way, which would lead to problems between her and Eloise. Ginny pouted. "The satin buttons look so good."

"Your silk buttons look good, too," Eloise countered.

"If we didn't own this shop, you wouldn't have so much choice. You would be like all of the other people who come to us. You'd request a few changes and be done with it," Ashleigh told her.

Ginny chewed her lip. "But the satin ones look more regal."

Eloise's face was like thunder. "You can't change anything

else on your dress. What do you think this is? A service just for you?"

Ashleigh was so tempted to give in. She was much harder on Eloise than she was on her youngest sister, and they all knew that. Ginny looked to her for support. Ashleigh shrugged. "Don't expect me to take sides. Eloise is right. We can't—*you* can't— keep making changes to your dress. What you have is beautiful, Ginny. You'll always see something newer and nicer. We don't have long to go, and you should hurry up and get things settled with your house. That should be your priority."

Ginny's wedding preparations were taking over their lives and she couldn't wait for the wedding to be over with and for Ginny to be off on her honeymoon. Ginny's fiancé, Ben, was another bone of contention between them all, though she and Eloise tried not to sound too negative in front of Ginny, especially now that things were definitely going forward.

Ashleigh wasn't impressed with him, and Eloise had said she had heard not so great things about him in his past, way before Ginny got involved with him. They had warned Ginny about all of this, but she had fallen head first in love like a fool, hard and fast. She'd paid no heed to their thinly veiled warnings. They hadn't been happy at all when Ginny announced that Ben had proposed, and that she had accepted.

There wasn't long to go before the wedding, and for now, focus was on Ginny, but soon enough, things would have to change. Ashleigh was ready for it.

Ginny narrowed her eyes. "You both pick on me all the time."

"We do not," she and Eloise replied in unison.

Ashleigh tried not to raise an eyebrow. "We give you everything you want." They had spoiled her too much. Ginny pulled out her phone as she and Eloise exchanged knowing looks.

"I'm taking my lunch break." Ginny stormed out of the shop.

Eloise smoothed out a dress on one of the mannequins. "No prizes for guessing who's she calling."

Ashleigh returned to replying to texts on her phone. "At least she'll be his problem soon." Then, realizing what she had said, "Ginny's not a problem, that's not what I meant."

"I know what you meant. She makes too many demands. If we owned a grocery store, we wouldn't have this problem."

"Truth," replied Ashleigh. This was most definitely true. *If.* There were too many 'ifs'. "But we'd probably have other problems."

They both laughed. Running an upscale bridal store was hard work, but rewarding, and seeing the look of pure joy on their customers as they tried on their dresses for the last time made everything worth it.

But life would have been so different 'if' their parents hadn't had that fatal car crash.

"She's getting antsy and nervous, maybe because there's not long to go. She'll be fine when she comes back from her honeymoon." At least, Ashleigh hoped so. She hoped that Ben would make Ginny happy. He seemed to. She was happy, and that was all that mattered.

"Have you considered what we'll do if Ginny decides she wants to go to work, like in an office or something? What if she wants to leave and get an ordinary job, working for a company, or something?" Eloise asked. Ashleigh looked up and stared at her sister's back. She hadn't considered that at all. It could very well be a possibility; one that could upset her own plans.

"We'll deal with that when it happens."

"You know I'm away at the same time?" Eloise asked. "After the wedding."

"For the first week only," Ashleigh clarified. Eloise's friend Beth, from college, was a rich Daddy's girl who lived in Hyannis

Port. She was getting married the week after Ginny, and Eloise had taken a week off for her wedding.

"Just the first week that Ginny is away," Eloise confirmed.

"I can cope for a week without you both here." Their part-time assistants were a great help.

"You and Ginny left me alone for a week or was it two weeks? Two years ago around Christmas time," Eloise reminded her.

"You're counting?" Ashleigh asked, surprised. She had held the fort so often that she was sure it amounted to more than a few months in duration. She remembered that time when she and Ginny had visited many places and negotiated with up-and-coming manufacturers and designers. It had been a worthy trip, and to her surprise, Eloise had managed quite well.

"I'm just saying."

Eloise was about to open her mouth to say more, but Ashleigh didn't care to listen. "I'll be in the office if you need anything." She picked up her notebook and pen, seeing that the shop was empty.

The coming weekend, Ginny and Ben were going to take care of some things for their new house which they had recently bought together but hadn't yet moved into. Ginny had been so excited about it, wanting to make a proper first home for her and Ben. They had been shopping together and had picked out the colors for the rooms and were now looking to buy kitchen wares and bedding.

Eloise's friend's bachelorette party was on Sunday—at least, one of the events was—and The Bridal Shop didn't open on Sundays. It was the one day the sisters all had off.

But Ashleigh was becoming increasingly sick and tired of her life running to a schedule. It wasn't just the schedule, or the shop, but the repetition of her daily life. Eloise reminding her just now of the week's vacation she'd be taking for her friend's wedding meant that she would be left taking care of things alone again.

It was almost as if her sisters didn't think she had a life.

She didn't.

Her life plans consisted of either meeting Darcie, her best friend since high school, doing her yoga in the backyard, enjoying little trips to various places, or the big highlight which was venturing out of state to find new suppliers.

The monotony was wearing thin. She hadn't been aware of it before, but for a few years now, a malaise had set in.

Her sisters carried on with their lives and, feeling left behind to shoulder all the burdens and responsibilities, a slowly simmering resentment was starting to boil over.

She needed to let them know now of her plans, but, also, *not* now.

Not *yet*.

Her plans for the future which she had started to put together had to be put on hold when Ginny had announced that she and Ben were engaged.

Ashleigh was the sensible one, the dependable sister, the one that the others relied on to fix things. It was precisely because she was all of these things that she was often left in the lurch.

If only she could be as spontaneous and happy-go-lucky as Eloise, and as sometimes selfish and naïve as Ginny.

She battled with when to tell them. Should she drop the bomb now? Break the news that she planned to take two or more months off to travel around Europe? Or should she let them know after the wedding?

If she told them before, she risked ruining the wedding for Ginny. So, she had resigned herself to waiting until Ginny returned from her honeymoon and Eloise from Beth's wedding.

She had waited all this time. She could wait a little longer. It was only a month and then her escape hatch would be open. She wouldn't be able to fly away immediately after telling them because there would be too many things to settle regarding the business. The last thing she wanted was to cause a disruption to her customers, but at least her sisters would know. And that would be a start.

Her intention would be out there, no longer a thought, unspoken and carried in her head, like invisible ink on a scrap of paper.

At forty-three years of age, it was time for *her* dreams to begin.

CHAPTER 3

They took their lunch in turns, and usually in their large office behind the shop floor. Ashleigh was supposed to meet her friend Darcie today but she had called to say she was busy, so Ashleigh took her lunch at her desk.

Ginny had returned having taken a longer lunch than usual, and Ashleigh stayed out of her way to avoid saying something that would hurt her. Pre-wedding nerves had settled in slightly sooner than expected, and Ginny was feeling especially fragile. Ashleigh and Eloise let her have as much time off as she needed in order to prepare for the wedding and get her new home in order, but they hadn't expected Ginny to start taking advantage of this so soon.

Eloise walked in, then hovered around looking for something on her desk. It was an unspoken rule that only one person at a time could be in the office, unless the shop was closed. But now, this was the second or third time that her sister had walked in, looking for something.

Ashleigh had been researching places to visit in Europe. It was similar to the trip she and Ford had planned all those years ago. She lowered her head, letting herself go back to that time for the tiniest of seconds. What a trip that would have been, and with the both of them so in love.

She shook her head, as if doing so might shake away those memories. She had detached herself from Ford soon after her parents' death. News of his marriage and the birth of a child a few years later had pricked her, short and sharp, like an injection, and then she had forced herself to forget all about him.

She clicked on a link which showed her places to visit in Greece and Italy. She didn't want to go on a cruise. The idea of being stuck on a ship, no matter how glamourous it was, did not appeal. Also, having to make friends just so that she could sit with someone for dinner and make small talk and polite conversation wasn't something she wanted to endure.

She looked up from her computer screen to find Eloise giving her an odd look, before she half turned to leave. Ashleigh blinked. Eloise was all fidgety, and her sister hardly ever fidgeted. It was a tell that Ashleigh knew well. She waited for her sister to spill the beans.

"What's Ginny gone and done now?" she asked finally, although she was sure that this—whatever it was—wasn't Ginny-related. Ginny prompted a different set of emotions in them both.

"Nothing." Eloise shuffled some papers on her desk. It was another tell. Her sister wasn't working; she was giving off the illusion of work.

"What are you looking for?" Ashleigh asked, needing her to be on the shop floor. Eloise scratched the back of her neck, the way she always did when she was usually holding something back.

"Has a customer canceled?" Ashleigh demanded. The expression on Eloise's face indicated that something like that had happened. It wasn't good when a customer canceled. Some did when a wedding fell through—and some did fall through in spectacular fashion for so many different and sometimes shocking reasons.

Eloise stared at her sheepishly. "No, no. Nothing like that. The, uh … you know I'm going to Beth's bachelorette party this weekend …"

She nodded. She knew, and she had it marked in her planner. It was supposed to be her Saturday off, but Ginny wasn't working that day either. She could manage, and Eloise would only be away from Saturday afternoon and returning on Monday morning. Hyannis Port was a five-hour drive from them. Apparently, Beth had planned a whole month's worth of weekend events for her bachelorette parties. Thankfully, Eloise was only going to the one this weekend.

"Uh … there's been a change of plans."

Ashleigh's insides hardened. "For what?" Eloise wasn't one to get nervous, so that fact that she was told her that this new plan was something she was going to hate.

"Beth has now decided that she wants to go to Vegas—"

Ashleigh's eyelids flew wide open. "Las Vegas?"

"For a longer weekend. She said because it's the only party that I can attend—"

"At least you can attend one. I can't imagine any working person being able to attend four weekends of bachelorette parties," said Ashleigh. Some people. Especially those who didn't have to work.

"So … uh … she wants to spend longer with me, and a few others. It's not only me that she's changing her plans for—"

"How nice for you both."

Her sarcasm wasn't lost on Eloise, who cocked her head. "She's my best friend. And it's Vegas. How can I not go?"

"The plan has changed from a meal and a spa day to a wild weekend in Vegas." Ashleigh didn't want to think about what they would get up to. She hung her head. Well, this was great, wasn't it? She was going to be burdened with working all by herself on Saturday.

It wasn't fair.

She never got a break.

She never did anything, and her sisters seemed to take full advantage of the fact that she did nothing, went nowhere, had no boyfriend and was there to keep things running while they gallivanted off.

"It's Beth's bachelorette party. I didn't have anything to do with the planning."

"Hit me with it, then. How much time do you want off?"

Eloise folded her arms. "We're meeting on Friday morning."

"*Friday morning*?" Which meant she'd probably get the early morning flight on that day. Eloise nodded, her expression indicating that she felt bad about this but Ashleigh could see right through it. She didn't feel *too* bad about it.

"When are you planning to come back?" She braced herself.

"On Monday evening." Her sister made a face as if it was painful to say this.

"When did the plans change?" Ashleigh demanded.

"A few days ago."

Ashleigh wiped a hand across her face, dismay and annoyance bubbling in her belly. "Why are you only telling me now?"

"I wanted to tell you this morning when I mentioned about taking a week off for the wedding. But I knew you'd be upset about it. I wasn't even sure I'd be going."

"Oh, come on, Eloise! How naïve do you think I am?"

"I knew you'd kick up a fuss, and I didn't know how to break it to you, and seeing how you're reacting, I was right." Eloise folded her arms even more tightly.

Ashleigh felt a tightness in her jawline. Why did her sisters always seem to make everything be her fault? Was she not entitled to a reaction?

"You're going, so don't pretend that you weren't sure you'd be going."

Eloise opened her mouth as if to protest, then seemed to think better of it and closed it.

"You should have told me as soon as you found out. You know it's starting to get busy around here. It's the least you could have done."

"You're mad at me because the plans have changed. I had no hand in changing them and I told you as soon as I could. You and Ginny will be here."

"Ginny and Ben are sorting out some things for the house. She's going out of town on Friday and Saturday." The Friday she could deal with, it was Saturdays that were the problem.

"If you're that mad about it, I'll leave late on Saturday night and be back home on Sunday night." Eloise stared at Ashleigh with her big brown eyes. "I'll go for a shorter time and miss the rest of it."

"To Las Vegas?" It wasn't possible, and Eloise knew that.

"I'll do it, if it makes you less grumpy," offered Eloise, but she knew, like Ginny did, that whenever something needed doing, or fixing, or someone needed to stay behind and hold down the fort, they all relied on Ashleigh. Just like now.

"No." Ashleigh's shoulders slumped in defeat. "I won't hear the end of it if I ruin your plans."

"Stop acting like a martyr."

"Really? Me? A martyr?" she scoffed.

"You do. You do this all the time, Ash. All the time."

Her sister stood up and walked over to her. "Do what?" She wasn't going to take this lying down. A martyr? She never played that pity card. "What do I do all the time, aside from stand in for when you or Ginny can't be here?"

"There you go again, blaming us because we have plans. If you had plans or wanted to do something, or needed to go away, we'd do the same for you. It's almost as if you're mad that we have a life."

Ashleigh's insides shook with rage. "What do you mean? *When* have I blamed anyone for having a life?"

"I can't spend my life being tied to this shop," Eloise cried, in a rare display of anger.

The words hit Ashleigh like bullets. "What? What do you mean?" Was Eloise thinking the same thing? The idea that her sister had also had enough, and possibly wanted a break, hit her like a sharp slap to her face.

"I have based my life around this shop," snapped Eloise. "We have to take turns to go on vacation, we don't always get the weekend off. It's always such a big deal when we need to take more time than we're allowed. I'm fed up with it all. I'd get a better deal working a nine-to-five job."

"You wouldn't make that much money." Ashleigh's heart slipped all the way down through her stomach, as if a rug had been pulled out from under her feet. *This* was how Eloise felt? She tried to recall how many times Eloise had been the one left taking care of the business alone.

Not many times at all. So, this was rich, coming from Eloise, and hearing her moan and complain about feeling so put upon.

"This is our job. This is what we do for a living," Ashleigh declared, fighting to keep her anger in check. "This is how we earn our money. This is what we live on."

"Don't you feel like it's taken over our lives?" Eloise cried. "Sometimes, I feel as if this place is an anchor and it's weighing me down. Sometimes I wish I wasn't tied to it."

Ashleigh bit her tongue. The truth was her sister had caught her unawares. She had been so busy thinking about her own plans for the future, and how they might affect everyone, that she had been treading on eggshells about when to tell them, and in one short sentence, Eloise had beaten her to it. It sounded as if her sister had had enough, too.

"It does get to be too much. I know. I feel the same," she replied, being truthful.

"I went to college and studied fashion design and for what?"

"For this," Ashleigh told her calmly. So many decisions had been made for them at such a young age. It wasn't just her own dreams that had been halted. She'd never thought of it like that before.

"I don't want to do this anymore," Eloise shot back. "We did this for Mom and Dad, and because we had nothing else to do but carry on, but this doesn't have to be our entire life. Just because we fell into it doesn't mean we have to do this until we die."

Ashleigh surveyed her sister's expressions and her heart dipped. She too wanted more, and as close as the sisters were in age, and as much as they were different in personality, it surprised her to discover that they both wanted the same thing at the same time.

A longing to escape.

Eloise's confession had come as a huge shock to her.

"I can't help it if Beth has changed the plans for her bachelorette party. I want to be able to get up and go to Las Vegas if that's what the new plan is. I want to be able to do what I want."

"You *do* do what you want."

"No, I don't. Not always."

"Name a time when you didn't." Ashleigh folded her arms. Why could they not see it? "This isn't the first time you've announced that something has come up, some friend you want to visit, some party, some ..."

"It's not my fault I have friends out of state. Someone had to go to college to study fashion."

"Or did you?" There was no real need to go to college.

Ashleigh had given up her dreams of pursuing a degree in journalism. Eloise had wanted to go to college, and Ashleigh and Aunt Becky had done their best to see that she could go and study. Not that it helped them much. Aunt Becky didn't have a college education, and she was able to do as much, when it came to alterations and changing small things on dresses, as Eloise did.

Their mother didn't have a college education either. She loved to sew and had a natural flair for fashion which she had grown stronger while she had worked in a bridal shop for a few years in New Hampshire, before meeting their father and settling further south in Whisper Falls. Here, with their father's encouragement and business know-how, they had taken the plunge and set up a small shop.

Eloise hadn't had to put her life on pause. She'd gotten her degree. She'd gotten married and divorced. She, more than any of the sisters, had been allowed to get up and go and be spontaneous. Without a doubt, Eloise pretty much did as she pleased, and Ashleigh wasn't going to sit here and let her sister make her feel guilty.

Ginny popped her head around the corner. "Am I the only one working here today? It's getting busy out there."

Eloise rushed and left, leaving Ashleigh staring at her computer, looking at a picture of the Trevi Fountain in Rome.

CHAPTER 4

"*E*loise said that?" Darcie squealed when Ashleigh finished telling her of their conversation a few days earlier.

"She did. She said that working at the shop doesn't have to be our life, and that just because we fell into it doesn't mean we have to do it until we die."

"You haven't told them, have you?"

"No."

"Still?"

"Still," Ashleigh replied.

"But now Eloise has told you how she feels. Don't be too surprised if she says she wants time out to go do her own thing."

"I'm trying to do the right thing," Ashleigh murmured, more to herself than to her friend. "Ginny's wedding isn't far off, and I figured I'd wait until after then."

"Then wait, and maybe Ginny will come back from her honeymoon and announce that she's pregnant, and Eloise will announce that she's leaving, and you'll have to come out of retirement and get back into working at the shop."

"Come out of retirement?" Ashleigh cried. "I'm not retiring. I only want to take some time off."

"What else will you do but make jam, and ..." Her friend shrugged. "I don't know. Whatever else you want to make."

"Is that what you think I've waited all these years to do, make stuff?" It surprised her that Darcie assumed she would stay here in Whisper Falls. She hadn't told Darcie of her plans to see Europe, and that was mainly because she hadn't yet decided fully what she would do. It was still a pipe dream until her sisters knew.

She had never been in the situation to do what she wanted. Well, she had once upon a time. With Ford, and a six-month trip to Europe, and dreams of living and studying in Boston, but that dream had ended before it had even started and she was fearful that something bad might happen again.

Her friend looked at her, then peered closer, as if she had suddenly realized there was a plan, and more. "What are you thinking? Do you have a plan?"

"I'm thinking that I'm forty-three years old and I have regrets."

"Regrets?"

Ashleigh peered down at her lap and scratched the material of her slacks. It wasn't easy to look at Darcie and say it. It wasn't easy to say it out loud at all, and now Eloise's admission earlier had shaken her up and she was feeling all out of sorts.

Darcie touched her arm. "Regrets about what, Ash?" she asked, quietly.

"Oh, you know, the usual."

"You mean Ford?"

She tilted her chin up quickly. "No. Not about Ford." Though she'd be lying if she said she never thought about him. She did, but not like *that*. He was married and had a child.

"Then what do you have regrets about?"

"Just … about me, being in my forties and having nothing to show for it."

"That's not true." Her friend snorted and stared at her in disbelief. "You have your sisters. You have the shop. You kept your mom and dad's business going, and you made it a big success."

"My parents would have made it a success."

"But maybe not like you have, Ash. You've expanded it and you've taken it to another level. People come here from miles around."

Ashleigh didn't see it quite like that. Darcie was being nice and supportive, because that was what friends did.

"I gave up everything, and now I want to do something for me," she said quietly.

"Like what, hon?"

Ashleigh looked at her friend for a long time, wondering whether to say it out loud, her dreams to travel, to leave the country and go abroad. She had money, and goodness knows she had been stuck in the same old town all her life. This hadn't been her plan at all when she had been starry-eyed with ambition.

"Like see the world."

"See the world?" Darcie picked up a potato chip and munched.

"There's so much of it to see."

"Since when have you wanted that—oh, *ohhhhhh*." Darcie leaned forward across the table where they were sitting having brunch. "Regrets about all the things you never got to do, the trip with Ford, those plans you made, is that what you're regretting?"

"I didn't intend to stay here for my entire life."

Her friend sat back and surveyed her. "You're not going to be making jam?"

"No. I don't even like jam. Why jam?"

"Doesn't have to be jam."

"Will you stop going on about the jam!"

"I never had you down for wanting to travel, Ash, that's all. This is the first I'm hearing about it, and I've known you all your life."

"I'm still trying to figure out what I want to do. I have ideas, too many of them."

"When were you going to tell me?" Darcie looked hurt.

"I haven't completely decided yet. I need to tell Eloise and Ginny that I need some time off, see how they take the news, and then I'll plan my trip. You know more than they do."

"I'm honored."

"You should be." It was okay for Darcie. She'd gotten married, then divorced then married a wonderful man and now had a teenage son.

Ashleigh had nothing like that, and as time went by, maybe also because Ginny, her baby sister, was getting married, she was beginning to realize that she had nothing solid, nothing that would remain, and it was making her uncomfortable. She was happy for Darcie, but her dreams had been halted and it was time to do something about them.

"Travel where?" Darcie asked, saying it in the tone of someone who thought she was clearly crazy for thinking such a thing.

"I haven't decided yet." She wasn't going to tell Darcie about Europe. Her dreams were flimsy, and she needed to protect them, most of all from people she loved, like Darcie and her sisters.

What would Eloise and Ginny make of it? She couldn't just up and leave. She needed to give them time to process this news. What she was doing was selfish, leaving them like this. What if they didn't want her to take so much time off? What if, as Eloise had shown recently, they felt hemmed in and stuck, too?

She was going off on a tangent again, forgetting the number of times the roles had been reversed. She was entitled to this. She wasn't doing anything wrong.

"I had something important to tell you today." Darcie sat forward looking all animated.

"What?"

Darcie's eyes grew large with anticipation.

"Well, tell me then," Ashleigh insisted, hating the wait. "What?"

"Speaking of Ford—"

"We weren't speaking about him."

"He's back, and rumor is, he's *divorced.*"

It was as if the air had slowly seeped out of her lungs. Ford still had family here and came home for Christmas and Thanksgiving sometimes. The last time she'd seen him was a few years ago, when his father had died. She'd seen him across the street with his wife and she had gone over to pay her respects.

"Aren't you going to say something?" Darcie raised her eyebrows expectantly.

Ford was divorced? The words still hadn't sunk in properly and she didn't know how she felt about that. She didn't know what to say.

"Like what?" Did Darcie expect her to jump up in glee?

"How do you feel? About him coming back, and him being divorced?"

She shrugged. "He's entitled to come back, it's his hometown."

"I specifically meant about him being divorced?"

"Darcie! It a sad situation. They have a child."

"Yes, I know, but is that all you've got to say?" her friend asked.

"What do you want me to say?"

"You have to talk to him."

"Why?"

"Why not? He's not married now."

"We split up decades ago, Darcie. We're different people now. I can't believe you're obsessed by the fact that he's divorced. He's probably heartbroken."

"You said you still wondered sometimes how it would be if the two of you had stayed together."

This was true. She had confided in Darcie a few times when she'd been in a self-pitying mood. How might things have been if her parents hadn't had that fatal car accident? If she hadn't had to change her plans. If she'd left this town and gone traveling with Ford for those six months. If she'd gone to Boston and gotten her journalism degree.

She would have been a different woman now with different ambitions and plans. She might not even have been with Ford, but she would have done the things she'd set out to do.

The 'what ifs' were making the fabric of the life she had already lived crumble before her eyes. This latest news about Ford returning, and being divorced, lit a match to that fabric and sent everything up in flames.

She recalled the first time she had heard that he'd gotten married, and then that he'd had a child. She had gotten over him by then, because she was the one who had pushed him away, but still, the pain twisted and sliced into her gut.

Theirs had been the purest, most raw, most wonderful kind of love set ablaze by their dreams and hopes, in a world that was full of possibility. They had both been young, idealistic, and with life's adventures lying in wait before them.

It was all so different now. In their forties, life wasn't over, but they weren't exactly young and ready to take on the world. Rather, they had both found their place within it. No longer was she infected by the same heady, exuberance of youth. What she felt was jaded, with a sense that she had left certain things too late, and that perhaps the time for doing certain things was over.

She was in the middle stage of her life, and she had to be careful about the choices she made.

This was why leaving Whisper Falls and exploring the world, even if it was just a small part of it, was probably the most exciting thing she would ever do.

CHAPTER 5

The sight of Eloise's wheeled duffel bag—white with palm trees—standing by the door made Ashleigh's gut clench.

Ginny came flying down the stairs, and Ashleigh's brow creased. Her sister was all dressed up in casual clothes, not the professional attire they wore when working at the shop. Had she missed something? "Where are you going?"

"There's a sale going on at the department store, thirty percent off bedroom furniture, and Ben said it would all go quickly so we had to be there."

Ashleigh didn't recall her sister telling her. As if reading her mind, Ginny cried, "I told you, and you said it would be okay."

"You did," confirmed Eloise, walking slowly down the stairs.

"With both of you taking so much time off, I hardly know what I'm saying 'yes' to anymore," Ashleigh snapped.

"I'll be back as soon as we get something. Hopefully by lunchtime," Ginny told her.

"In that case, I'll see you when I get back," Eloise hugged her.

"You won't see us before then, will you?" Ginny replied sarcastically.

"Don't go getting any ideas about jetting off to Las Vegas for *your* bachelorette party," Eloise told her as Ginny opened the door to leave.

Ginny threw an odd glance over her shoulder. "You said we were keeping it local."

"We did?" Ashleigh and Eloise stared at one another in guilt. They had briefly talked about Ginny's bachelorette party a few weeks ago, but things had turned hectic. Work had been so full on and they hadn't done a thing since then, although they had penciled in the date into their calendars. Ginny's event was the week before the wedding and on the same weekend that Ben was having his bachelor party.

"You're just pretending you haven't organized it," said Ginny. "Have fun!"

"I intend to," Eloise replied.

"I'll be at the shop as soon as I can," Ginny told Ashleigh before disappearing and leaving just the two of them in the hallway. Eloise pulled out the handle of her duffel bag and glanced at her watch. "The cab should be here soon. Are you going to be okay by yourself for two days?"

You're worried about that now?

"I think I can handle things by myself," Ashleigh retorted.

"We forgot Ginny's bachelorette party. Did you do anything for it?" Eloise asked.

"Did *you*?"

"I forgot. I thought you might have …"

"Why am I always expected to do everything?" Ashleigh walked away into the kitchen to get her morning cup of coffee, muttering to herself under her breath.

Eloise followed her in. "That's all we hear from you lately, Ash. I only asked you a question. There's no need for you to get all worked up about it. If you're that mad at me for going and leaving you, then I'll stay. I'll tell Beth something came up and—"

"You're not going to do that. You've called the cab and you're ready to go."

"I can cancel it."

Ashleigh took a seat at the table. "That won't be necessary. What are we going to do about Ginny's bachelorette night?"

"You said you'd take care of it," Eloise reminded her. Ashleigh couldn't remember given the amount of things she had to constantly juggle in her head.

"I'm sure I meant *we'd* take care of it." Even though that probably wasn't what she'd said. It was no one's fault but her own because she always automatically assumed all responsibility. Could she blame her sisters for not pulling their weight when she didn't give them a chance?

She rubbed her forehead. "Sorry, I completely forgot. I can't even remember what we decided."

"We decided that we'd have a few spa treatments at The Connington and make use of their amenities."

"Now that I recall, it was something like that." The Connington was an opulent and old-fashioned hotel, and the spa center was an oasis of bliss.

"Ginny couldn't stop going on about the pool when she went to her friend's party there. Don't you remember?"

"I remember. I'll get onto it."

Eloise pulled out a chair and sat down. "*I'll* do it. I'll have time to arrange it this weekend. You've got enough on your hands."

"You've finally realized?" Ashleigh mumbled. She was beginning to feel sorry for herself, the palm trees on the duffel signaled a sense of adventure, something that she was hungry for.

"I should have realized that it's going to be harder for you, what with Ginny traipsing around and dealing with her preparations." Eloise air quoted 'preparations.'

"Leave her. She's getting married. It's about time one of the Rose sisters had a happy wedding and a happy ever after."

"I had a happy wedding," Eloise shot back. "It's the happy ever after that eluded me."

"I'm expecting her house to look like a show home, with the amount of time the two of them have spent on it."

They had helped the couple, along with Ben's parents, with the deposit for the house. It was a small two-bedroom home about a thirty-minute drive from their family home. She and Eloise had only seen it a few times in the beginning, along with Ben and Ginny who had talked about their plans and how they were going to decorate it.

"Don't expect too much," Eloise cautioned. "Ginny said they've had quite a few disagreements over the wallpaper and paint. And even some of the furniture."

"They're going to have to reach a compromise."

The sound of a horn tooting outside made Eloise stand up quickly. "That's my cab to the airport."

Ashleigh stood up. "Don't rub it in."

"I'm sorry for leaving you like this," Eloise said, as they hugged.

"No, you're not." There was a big grain of truth in that, but she smiled as she said it, hoping to take the edge off the irritation she felt. "Go, go and have fun. You can make up for it when you come back."

She walked with her sister and opened the door. Eloise grasped the long handle of her bag. Ashleigh watched the palm trees sail out of the house.

CHAPTER 6

*E*loise left the house and felt the weight of world melt away from her shoulders. The cab driver helped her put her bag into the trunk and she slid into the back seat, her thoughts fixed firmly on the fun-filled weekend ahead of her.

Las Vegas!

She was fired up beyond belief. She'd been to Vegas only once in her life before, when she was at college, and her group of friends had spent a few days there after final exams.

Going there now felt a bit like that, as if she was escaping from something—not final exams but something just as heavy and constricting.

Life with her sisters was becoming more like that. It never used to be. Returning to the family home after her short marriage had failed had been comforting. There was a warmth and familiarity about the home she had grown up in, and the three of them, along with Aunt Becky until her passing, had happy, glorious memories of it.

But lately, in the last few years, something had changed. Ashleigh had become more moody, more emotional, and made Eloise feel that everything was her fault. She tried to figure out when it had started. Had it been last year, after Ginny had announced her engagement, that things had started to change? Ashleigh seemed more temperamental than ever, frustrated and unhappy. And she rarely found fault with Ginny, though as her wedding day got closer, Ginny seemed to be trying everyone's patience. But Ginny would leave soon, and even though she would continue to work at the bridal shop, at least she would have her own life and her own place.

Were she and Ashleigh destined to spend the rest of their lives together, in this house, growing old together? Being those sisters who only had each other, and a few cats, for company.

Working alongside her sisters had been fun, and she looked forward to it every day, talking to giddily happy new brides-to-be and helping them to find the perfect dresses for their perfect day.

But that passion and excitement was wearing off. She didn't use much of her degree, hardly any of it, but she had a flair for art and creativity, and she could sketch what they wanted, and then work with designers, if need be, to create the perfect dress.

She looked out of the car window, grateful for this latest change of plans for Beth's event. It highlighted how desperate she was to leave.

She wasn't going to leave The Bridal Shop just yet. She wasn't going to worry about any of that now. Instead, she pushed all these negative thoughts to the back of her mind and sealed them away. She would worry about them another day.

This weekend, she was going to have some fun.

CHAPTER 7

They had managed to get a good deal on the bedroom dressers and beds. They had left this until the end, after all the painting was done. There was some painting to finish off in the guest bedroom, but other than that, their new home was almost complete. Ginny couldn't wait to be married and living there with Ben.

Luckily, they had finished their errand early enough for her to return to the shop before lunchtime. She could sense that Ashleigh wasn't in a great mood, probably because Eloise was away for the weekend as well.

It didn't help that Ginny was taking Saturday off, and she knew that this was why Ashleigh was more grumpy than usual. Come to think of it, Ashleigh had been like this ever since Ginny had announced that she and Ben were getting married. Maybe the pressure of the wedding preparations was becoming stressful for her family?

For that reason, she wanted the wedding over and done with so that she could begin her new life. And, she hoped, it might make Ashleigh return to her former and more pleasant self.

Ginny made sure she worked diligently all day, so that her sister wouldn't get too irked about her taking a day off tomorrow.

Early the next morning, she quickly bade Ashleigh a hurried 'bye' and rushed out. Ben was waiting outside for her, She slipped her overnight bag into the back of the car before climbing in. "Hi." She leaned over to give him a kiss, but he was busy looking at his cell phone, texting.

A tiny surge of disappointment shot through her veins. Things between them had been easygoing and more fun when they had been dating. Lately, Ben was more intense and short-tempered. The wedding pressure seemed to be affecting him as much as it was Ashleigh.

As for herself, she was so happy and relaxed about it all, and she didn't understand what the stress was about.

"Hi," she said again, waiting patiently for him to finish what he was doing. She'd been so looking forward to seeing him again. This was what pure love was like; it made it impossible to be away from him for more than a few hours. She was soppily, ridiculously in love.

Ben finally looked up. "Hey, babe." He put his phone away and dropped a kiss on her cheek. "You're late."

"How can I be late? You said eight o'clock."

He drove off, then turned to her with an apologetic expression. "I have to work half a shift today."

"What? No! Why didn't you tell me?"

"I'm telling you now."

"Ben." She couldn't keep the disappointment out of her voice and as she stared straight ahead, her happiness quickly deflated. "I could have helped Ashleigh at the shop. She's going to be really busy today, and Eloise is out of town."

"Where's she gone?"

"To her friend's bachelorette party in Las Vegas."

"Vegas? Wow. She sure knows how to party in style."

"Her friend is rich."

"You don't have to be rich to go to Vegas, you just have to be ready to party."

Ginny glanced at him, wondering if he felt envious. A couple of times he'd mentioned to his friends, in front of her, that he was too young to settle down. His words had sunk through her skin and settled into her heart, like thorns. When she'd later broached him about it, he'd kissed her and hugged her, and won her over with his sweet talking, telling her that this was how guys talked. He didn't mean it. He loved her.

"She's getting married the week after us," she said.

"Yeah?" He slowed the car down to a halt. "Want me to drop you off at the shop? I can pick you up when I'm done."

She could, but she didn't want to put Ben out, driving her here and there, and the poor man was working too. Besides, Ashleigh had told her that she could take time off for the wedding. If only Ben had called and told her this morning, before he'd come by.

"I can finish up the painting, or anything else at the house while I wait," she suggested, wanting to make herself useful. If she'd known, she would have come in appropriate clothing. They had planned for today to be a shopping and lunch day, and she had dressed accordingly but her white slacks and a printed white top wouldn't do for the task she now had.

He started up the engine again. "That's a good plan. There are a couple of walls in the second bedroom that need painting."

"Weren't we going to shop for your tie, cufflinks and shoes?" She had spent weeks, if not months, looking for ideas for her dream wedding dress and had carefully planned how she would do her hair. She had also picked her shoes and accessories to match. Ben was going to wear a normal suit, and he still hadn't gotten everything for the big day. Sometimes the differences between them seemed greater than the parts they had in common.

"Let's finish the painting, and tomorrow we'll go shopping for the other stuff we need."

She hadn't planned on spending the day painting, and on her own, but if that's what today was going to bring, she'd do it.

"You should have called and told me about the change of plans, Ben."

"Are you mad at me?"

"I was looking forward to going shopping and having lunch with my fiancé somewhere."

He glanced her way and gave her that sexy smile she loved so much. "We can do that tomorrow."

CHAPTER 8

*S*he was mad. Not raging mad, not like a bull about to drive its horns into something, but she was quietly angry as she walked around the shop at the end of the day adjusting and checking the wedding dresses that were on the mannequins, making sure nothing had been snagged, and there were no dirty marks left on them.

One of the assistants was sweeping the floor.

They hadn't been this busy in months. Springtime was busy for weddings. All she wanted was to go home and collapse on the sofa, preferably with a glass of Chardonnay.

"Hey, Ash."

A tingle spread through her from top to toe, before the air whooshed right out of her lungs. She would recognize that voice anywhere. It was a voice she hadn't heard, not in such close proximity, not saying her name like that, for a long time.

She turned around and found herself looking into Ford Montgomery's azure blue eyes.

Good lord. The man had aged most beautifully. The slim and angular-faced boy she had fallen hook, line and sinker for had transformed into a man with broad shoulders and a strong jaw.

His twinkling eyes looked into her and through her, and the wrinkles around them made him more handsome. She forgot to breathe for a few moments, staring into that handsome face of his which had only become more weathered and attractive over time. The boyish good looks were gone, but that lethal combination of dark brown hair—of which he still had plenty—and eyes that still had the power to mesmerize her, those things remained the same as she remembered.

The result was nothing short of jaw-dropping.

It flashed past her, all the highs and the lows; the things he'd said that made her laugh, the things which broke her heart, the letters they'd written, the ones that slowly fizzled away. And now he had walked back into her life as if it was the most normal thing in the world for him to do.

"Ashleigh?" He took a few steps towards her, peering at her until she realized she hadn't said a word.

"Ford …" She tried to take a few steps towards him, but her legs were so wobbly, she was afraid her knees might buckle and she'd fall. "What are you doing here?"

"Uh … just looking around …"

Darcie had said that he was divorced, or maybe he was getting divorced? She couldn't trust rumors. She had to hear it from him. She looked around, in case he'd walked in with someone, maybe a new fiancé, or someone who was looking for a wedding dress.

"I'm about to lock up, but I can stay open for a while longer if you need to look around."

Amusement danced in his eyes. "I'm not looking for a dress. I came to see you."

"Me?" Her insides were in turmoil. How could he still have this effect on her now after all this time? It had been so long since they had last stood together in a room, only the two of them, that she didn't know how to be. She almost placed her hand on her chest, but sense prevailed, and she stood upright.

Just because she was falling apart inside didn't mean that he had to see it.

They had split up and that had been the end of it. Him coming to her shop, looking for her today, well, that was just frightening, and unexpected, and exciting, all at the same time.

"It's … it's … it's nice to see you again," she stammered "It's been so long. What brings you here?" She tried to look busy, smoothing down the dress of the mannequin nearest to her; tried to look unaffected and casual—as if she didn't care for his words—but she was failing and he could probably tell, because he knew her better than any man ever had.

"I was passing by. I wanted to say 'hi'."

She tried to suppress a grin. Because that was a pure lie. Nobody passed The Bridal Shop on their way to someplace else. They had moved out of the center of town to further out, so that anyone coming to the shop was doing so because they wanted to come here.

"Hi," she replied, giving an awkward little laugh and hating herself for her sudden loss of poise.

He cleared his throat. "Are you free?"

She blinked and then cocked her head as if she had misheard. "Free for?" she almost choked, as a frog caught in her throat and held there. Ford Montgomery was asking her if she was free for what? Food, a drink, life?

"I mean, as in you're not busy? Am I getting in the way?" He looked around.

"No, you're good. It's the end of the day, and we're closing up."

"It's been a while."

"It has." She laughed nervously. She had stopped thinking about this man the moment she's learned he'd gotten married. She had somehow managed to wean herself off him, and she had been clean for all those years.

"I wanted to catch up with you." His eyes twinkled under the light of the chandelier.

Her heart seemed to be doing a little jig inside her chest. "About what?"

"About what?" he echoed, his brows twisting at her words. "Things. Life happened, and we drifted apart, but I've always wondered how you were, Ash. What happened to you was the worst thing. I should have been better."

Had he already alluded to them being together, and then splitting up as well as the thing-that-had-changed-her-life? "Things got busy." She tucked a lock of hair behind her ear. "You had a career to follow."

"But I should have been a better support."

"I'm the one who told you to go," she reminded him. Why was he bringing this up now? It had been a long time since they had spoken face to face, just the two of them, since she had told him there was no future for them, that she wouldn't ever come to Boston, and that he should carry on without her. To go from that to this was so jarring, it almost felt like whiplash. "I wouldn't have let you put your dreams on hold for me."

"I know, but it still feels wrong that I left and you stayed behind and …"

"I had things to take care of."

He looked around, his gaze taking in everything, with his hands in his pockets, and dressed in a pale blue shirt with the top button undone, he was still as handsome as ever. "You've done an amazing job with this place."

"Thank you. It happened slowly, over the years. I like to think my mom and dad would have been pleased."

"They would have," he said softly. His eyes turning shiny then. "They most definitely would have."

"Aunt Becky didn't get to see the new refurb." She gestured with her hand to the chandeliers and the chaise lounges.

"That's a shame. She would have loved it. She was proud of you girls."

Ashleigh smiled. Aunt Becky had been a strong support for them in their time of need, and Ashleigh liked to think that she and her sisters had done the same for her, nursing her as well as they could have and being by her side when she got sick and passed away.

"I got the upscale vibe as soon as I walked in," said Ford, walking around, taking a good look at the décor and the mannequins. "I kept meaning to come in and see it, see you and Eloise and Ginny, but I … it didn't seem right. Susan, my wife … my ex-wife …"

She couldn't tell if that was a smooth but deliberate reference to his status, or whether he was being genuine. Maybe he was being both, but she was unsure, and still trying to deal with him being here now like this.

"There are things I meant to say to you, Ash, to tell you, and us finishing the way we did, it didn't seem right."

"I broke it off."

"I shouldn't have let you." He'd waited a year, thinking she would finally join him, but how could she have left her sisters behind to start a new life when the life that they had known had been so brutally crushed? When he'd told her he was going to return to Whisper Falls, she broke up with him, telling him that she had responsibilities and more pressing matters to deal with. She didn't have time for romance and never would.

It had been so hard early on when she'd had a toddler Ginny to contend with, as well as a teen Eloise with all her angst and temper tantrums. Aunt Becky had been strong, standing in, taking over, being a mom and dad to them all, but it was Ford who had been her rock in the initial days, when the shock of losing her parents in such a way had broken her. She'd had to keep a strong face and demeanor, because she couldn't crumble when Eloise was sobbing, or when Ginny cried herself to sleep, screaming for her mommy.

Ashleigh had soldiered on, crying quietly alone at night in her room, or in Ford's arms during the precious little time they'd had together.

The responsibility of her sisters and the business, even with Aunt Becky by her side, was all-consuming. She couldn't imagine a life with anyone just then, so she'd broken up with him.

It had broken her heart to write that letter, but she had done it because it was the best thing for them both.

"You don't have to talk about that now, Ford. It's in the past."

He shook his head. "No, I do. I do." He fell silent for a while. "I couldn't do it before."

Because he was married?

"It's done now, and it all worked out fine," she said, wishing that her voice wouldn't sound so shaky.

"So, you never got married?"

Was that a question, or a statement? She wasn't sure.

"I never married, no. You have a daughter, I heard." He hadn't wasted much time in getting married and starting a family.

"Maddie. She's a great kid."

"That's nice." Ashleigh didn't know what to say to that. All she could think of was that he had a child. He had something to show for his life, while she had remained here the entire time with nothing to show for it. The business her mother had so lovingly started was beginning to feel more and more like an anchor around her neck.

"You never met anyone?"

His question surprised her. It was pointed and personal, especially after they'd spent so much time apart, and had cut off contact with one another for the past twenty years aside from the time when she'd briefly paid her respects after his father's death.

"Why are you asking me all these questions, Ford?"

He shoved his hands in his pockets, his jaw jutting out strong and prominent, as he stared at her. "I just want to catch up, Ash. We split up but I always wondered how things were going for you."

"Are you still open?"

They both turned towards the door. A woman had walked into the shop, looking none too pleased.

"I was about to close the shop, but, sure, we can still stay open for a while." It was twenty minutes past closing time, and the only reason the shop door was still open was because Ford had walked in and she'd lost all track of time. She couldn't turn this woman away. They never turned anyone away.

"My dress doesn't fit properly. It's too loose. Please, you need to fix it."

"Of course. Let me take a look." The woman carried the oversized garment carrier carefully over to her.

"See you around some other time, Ash." There was a softness in Ford's eyes that she remembered from before. Staring at him now, she was reminded of the twenty-five-year-old she had loved and lost.

"'Bye," was all she could manage as she ushered her customer towards one of the chaise lounges and listened to the woman's woes. Her wedding was coming up and she had lost a lot of weight in between picking up the dress a few weeks ago and now. The woman explained that the dress was too loose. After helping her to get into the dress, Ashleigh could see for herself the problem. She tried to calm her down as she took her measurements and promised her that the dress would be fixed in time for the wedding which was two weeks away.

"I'll come here next week," the woman said. "I want to come here and try it on and then I'll feel confident."

"That's perfectly fine," Ashleigh assured her as she scribbled down the measurements, her heart still skittering around in her ribcage at the fact that Ford had been here to see her.

Her reaction to him had been too extreme, and she didn't do extreme. Ginny did. Eloise sometimes, too. Ashleigh did not. Yet, she felt out of sorts. She hadn't felt lightheaded, like *this*, a ditzy teenager in love, since she had been of that age.

It didn't sit well with her, that Ford Montgomery had walked into her shop and into her life, declared that he now had an ex-wife, and had the temerity to ask her how she was doing.

Why did he need to know? And why had he come to her shop at the end of the day when the chances were high that she would be locking up to go home?

She called Darcie as soon as she got home. "Ford came by." She was breathless, as if she'd run a mile, which clearly didn't make sense given that she'd seen him over an hour ago and had driven home.

"He did, huh?" Darcie sounded laidback, but her own insides were on fire.

"Didn't you hear me? Ford came back, *my* Ford, I mean, not *my* Ford, but *Ford*."

"I knew who you meant."

"Can you meet up?" she asked, though it sounded more like begging. She needed someone to talk to about it. She needed her friend.

"Hon, I wish I could. I can hear that you're all fired up—"

"I am not."

"Yes, you are. But Eric has cooked dinner, and yes, while I may be blessed that he can and he did, he's made a big mess in the kitchen and I can't walk away without cleaning it all. I won't even enjoy eating what he's made because of the mess."

"Sure, okay. Tomorrow? What about lunch? Or brunch?" Sooner would be better. "Can you meet me for brunch?"

"Brunch sounds good," said Darcie.

She wouldn't sleep tonight. Even now, telling Darcie about her encounter, her stomach was churning. She couldn't explain her reaction to him nor understand why she was behaving like a love-struck teenager.

Well, maybe she could, a little. Her reaction might have had something to do with the lack of romance in her life in recent years.

CHAPTER 9

*S*he managed to sleep, eventually, but on waking up the first thing she thought of was Ford.

Irritated by this, and not understanding why she couldn't get this man out of her mind given the fact that he had been out of her mind for so many years, she got out of bed and did some yoga outside in her backyard.

Bathed by the sunshine and standing in the middle of nature, with only the trees and greenery to look at, she felt a sense of calm that had eluded her. Yoga grounded her and took her mind off things as she held her pose and breathed in deeply.

Afterwards, she sat on a patio chair drinking iced tea, feeling rejuvenated and refreshed.

With her mind in a calmer state, she came to the conclusion that her fascination and obsessiveness over Ford was due to a void in her life. She hadn't dated for over a year, and even when she did date, it didn't last for too long. It never went anywhere.

It wasn't that she had broken up with her boyfriends because she was hung up on Ford. She wasn't. She had moved on. Her past romances hadn't worked out because the men she met didn't make her *feel*. There was fun and laughter to be had. Some intimacy. Companionship and the removal of loneliness, but it had never been enough for her to meet anyone and think that he was 'the one.'

Deep in thought, she heard a sound. Like a door closing. Then she assumed she must have been imagining it. But at the sound of footsteps rushing up the stairs, her heart almost jolted from her chest.

Startled, she got up and walked inside only to find Ginny's bag lying at the bottom of the stairs.

"Ginny?" She called up the stairs.

No answer.

She walked upstairs and knocked on her sister's door. She hadn't expected Ginny to come home until later this evening because her sister had told her that she and Ben had a few things to do during the day. She knocked again.

"Ginny?" Was that the sound of crying? Alarmed, she opened the door to find Ginny lying on the bed hugging a pillow. Her sister's bloodshot eyes and blotchy face were a shock to her system.

She rushed to her side. "What's wrong? What happened?"

"We had a fight."

Ashleigh sat down and placed a hand on her sister's hip. "Over what?" This wasn't the first time that Ben had upset Ginny. She was sensitive, no doubt about that, but some of the things they had fought about had raised alarm bells in both her and Eloise. "What happened this time?"

Ginny sat up, hugging her knees and throwing the pillow to the side. This wasn't good, with not long left until the wedding.

She listened as Ginny told her how they'd gone shopping to order some lamps and finishing pieces and how she'd had her heart set on one particular style of lamp but Ben hadn't liked it.

She did, and this time she wasn't going to back down, so she confronted him about it, about why he always had the last word on their decisions, which were supposed to be jointly made. Ginny's lower lip started to tremble. "He got mad, and started saying things …"

Ashleigh put her arms around her and held her tightly. "What sort of things?" she whispered, a part of her aching with fear, and the other part boiling with rage.

"He said I always got what I wanted, and that I was spoiled, and that you two let me have my way but he wasn't going to."

"Sounds to me as if he always gets his way," countered Ashleigh, loosening her embrace and moving away in order to give Ginny some space. Something twisted in her gut and she found it increasingly difficult to see Ben favorably. Ginny was marrying this guy and Ashleigh didn't like him. There was no easy way to say it, and the closer the wedding date seemed to be, the more Ben seemed to make Ginny's life miserable.

She and Eloise were both fearful for Ginny. What would Mom and Dad have done? What advice would they have given Ginny? Ashleigh was still old enough to have memories of her parents, but Ginny didn't. She had been so young. Ashleigh hugged her sister again, knowing that she was the only mother figure Ginny had. She had to give Ginny her all.

"He doesn't always get his way," Ginny sniffled. Ashleigh had to bite her tongue and not say the wrong thing, but there was nothing to say but the truth; that Ben was a bully, and that he didn't deserve anyone like Ginny. Her sister had a petulant side, but she was also kind and loving. Ashleigh kept her arms wrapped around her and wished she knew the right things to do and say. "I don't like that he's upset you."

"What am I going to do?" Ginny's voice was tiny.

Ashleigh pulled away. "What do you want to do?" She wiped

her sister's tears with the back of her hand, then got up and fetched a box of tissues.

"I don't know."

"We'll support you whatever you decide."

"Support me?" Ginny blew her nose and stared up at her quizzically. "It was just a lamp. I don't need to make a big deal about it. He's having a tough time at work, and they keep making him work crazy hours. He's under pressure."

"Welcome to the real world," Ashleigh muttered under her breath. But she was thinking of the bigger picture, the bigger *problem*. If Ben was like this about home furnishings, who knew what problems lay ahead for Ginny? Fear and worry sank into her chest, the heaviness weighing down her entire body. How could she be happy for Ginny when she believed her sister was making a mistake? His parents and family were nice enough, but Ginny was going to spend her life with Ben, not his family. Her gut roiled just thinking about it.

"Why don't you wash your face, and come downstairs, and I'll make you some of your favorite pancakes. Blueberry ones, just how you like." She tucked a lock of Ginny's hair behind her ear.

"I'd like that." Her sister's face lit up, but her eyes were still sad. "Did you have any plans? Were you going to go to the farmers' market or something?"

"No. No plans. Get up and wash your face. Wipe away the tears, then come down when you're ready. I'll get started."

"Thanks."

Ashleigh closed the door behind her and leaned against it. She would have to call Darcie and tell her that brunch was off. This was far more important than sitting with her friend, discussing the re-entry of Ford Montgomery into her world.

She set about making the pancakes. A short while later Ginny came down, looking fresher and a little more composed. Her eyes brightened at the sight of the pancakes and the bowl of blueberries and jug of maple syrup. Ashleigh had also brewed a fresh pot of coffee. They sat down and ate together and Ashleigh talked about everything and anything except Ben.

It was fine if Ginny wanted to talk about him, but until then, Ashleigh kept the conversation on other things, which was difficult, given that she couldn't talk about anything in the bridal shop, or Eloise, who was at a bachelorette party.

Did Ginny have doubts? It was wishful thinking on Ashleigh's part, and this wasn't the first time such a thing had crossed her mind. Eloise also felt this way, but the two of them hadn't sat and discussed this subject in such clear terms.

"How am I going to be happy if we can't agree on the simplest of things?" Ginny asked, as she heaped a spoonful of blueberries onto her plate. "A lamp. We argued over a lamp."

Okay, so maybe her sister did want to talk about this.

"Do you argue a lot?"

"Lately, it seems like all we do is argue. We argue about the honeymoon, about the dress."

"What about the dress?" The dress was none of Ben's business. And besides, Ginny's dress was beautiful. She couldn't see why he would have a problem with the dress.

"He said he didn't want it to show too much skin."

Ashleigh's eyes almost popped right out of their sockets. "It's nothing to do with him," she said, because the type of dress Ginny wanted to wear was up to her. Ginny's dress showed off more of her back than was usual, but it wasn't too low. But still, this little matter about Ben not wanting her to expose too much skin now had her worried. She tried to compose herself even as warning signs went off in her head. Ginny's fiancé was beginning to sound too controlling.

Why had she never noticed this before?

Had she missed a sign?

Other than the fact that her insides tightened every time she was left in the room with him, there was nothing concrete she could say about him to Ginny. But these things were starting to come out now. They could be attributed to the stress of the wedding, but she was worried that it might be more than that.

This was a colossal failure on her part not to see Ben for the type of man he was. A man didn't become controlling overnight. Guilt started to gnaw in her stomach. She had missed these things, and she should have looked out for her sister more. Their parents would have spotted these signs sooner, of that she was sure.

"What did you tell him about the dress?"

"I didn't. It won't matter what he thinks because we'll be at the church by the time he sees me in my dress. What's he going to say to me then?"

Her sister's naivety alarmed her. If fighting over a lamp had reduced Ginny to tears and upset her so much that she'd had to rush home, Ashleigh didn't want to think about what might happen at the church when Ben saw her dress.

She wasn't convinced that he would keep his mouth shut and say nothing. In fact, she was more certain than ever that he would do the opposite and cause a scene on their wedding day and break Ginny's heart.

And if that happened …

The doorbell rang, and she got up to answer it. She wasn't expecting any visitors. But when she opened the door and stared into Ben's thin, long face, her insides jolted as if she'd been tasered.

"Ben." She tilted her head, confusion and anger mincing together and hardening her face. "What do you want?"

"I've come to see Ginny. I lost my temper and I didn't mean to."

"She doesn't want to see you." Ashleigh closed the door a

little and stepped out, forcing Ben to take a step backwards. "You upset my sister a *lot*."

"I didn't mean to."

"I don't care whether you meant to or not. You did," she thundered, while trying to keep her voice low.

"I need to talk to her."

"That's not a good idea."

"I don't care what you think. It's Ginny I want to speak to."

Her stomach hardened, as if concrete had been injected into it. This no-good piece of dirt would have to fight her first. "I don't care what you want to do," she growled. "You will not speak to Ginny today."

"Ben." Behind her, Ginny's voice wasn't tinny and small anymore. It was full of hope and reconciliation. Ashleigh ground her teeth. Ginny had caved in.

Again.

Ben stepped around Ashleigh and reached out with his hand, pulling Ginny out towards him. "I'm sorry, babe." He put his arms around her and kissed her. "It's only a goddamn stupid lamp. I shouldn't have lost my temper."

"It was a stupid lamp." Ginny let go of his hand, and Ashleigh wished her sister would develop a spine and hold out instead of giving into this bully like a wet fish.

"I went back and bought it for you, and the other things you liked. The butter dish, and the plate set, and the mugs."

"You did?" Ginny's eyes gleamed with joy, and these words instantly erased all the bad memories from earlier as the two of them hugged and kissed.

Ashleigh turned and left them to it. Back in the kitchen, she sat back down at the table and stared at the stack of pancakes, and the almost untouched one on Ginny's plate along with the blueberries.

Footsteps in the hallway made her muscles clench. "We're

going shopping," Ginny announced. Her demeanor had changed so quickly, it gave Ashleigh more cause for worry. Ben stood by her, a gloating expression across his face.

"I told her I was sorry. She knows I didn't mean to get so mad."

"Does she?" Ashleigh looked at him with eyes as hard as flint.

"I love her, and I'm stressed working all these crazy shifts at the factory."

"We all have to work," muttered Ashleigh. "That's no excuse for being rude and nasty."

"He said he's sorry, Ashleigh, can we let it go?" Ginny looked at Ben with puppy-dog eyes, as if she would follow him to the ends of the Earth, and to Hell if need be. "I'm sorry about the pancakes. I'll have them when I come back."

Ashleigh slumped back in her seat. "Whenever."

"I'm taking you to dinner," said Ben. "You won't have any room for pancakes."

"Aren't you the lucky one?" Ashleigh snapped at him. Ginny came over and started to clear her dishes.

"Don't worry about the dishes, or the pancakes. You go enjoy your day."

"Are you sure?" Ginny kissed her on the top of her head, something she rarely did. At some level, Ashleigh presumed, even Ginny knew that she'd messed up Ashleigh's day.

"I'm sure."

"Thanks. See you later."

The door closed and silence fell, as heavy as the disappointment that swam inside her. Ashleigh stared at the stack of pancakes and the almost full bowl of blueberries.

Another wasted day for her, with her plans in tatters. It was too late to meet Darcie for brunch. She wasn't in the mood to meet her later, either. This whole episode with Ben had soured her mood. She couldn't get angry at Ginny, even though the disappointment was heavy.

She got up and started clearing away the dishes, and then it dawned on her what she would do later. She would surf the net and continue with her travel plans, and maybe next week, she would tell her sisters. Sooner than she'd intended.

CHAPTER 10

On Monday morning, Ginny was sitting at the table eating breakfast as normal, as if everything was right with the world again.

"Everything okay?" Ashleigh asked, wanting to make sure.

"Peachy." Ginny set down her coffee cup, pondering before saying. "Ben's really not that bad. I've made him out to be some sort of selfish monster but he's not like that. It's me. I'm too sensitive. Ben says I'll grow out of it."

"Is that what he says?" Ashleigh had a good mind to give that boy a few home truths about himself.

"I love him," Ginny gushed happily, as if nothing bad had happened. "I love him and I'm going to be his wife. Things will be better."

"Things will be *better*?" Ashleigh's insides squeezed together and she missed having Eloise around so that she could share her troubles with her. Things were supposed to be good already now, not at some time in the future.

She had been younger than Ginny when she and Ford had made plans for a life in Boston, and though they hadn't talked about marriage, she knew it was something that would happen one day, that they would take that step. She hadn't hoped or prayed that things would be better, because she already had a wonderful relationship with him. He had been strong, but kind, focused on his career, and yet with all the time in the world for her. He'd made her feel special, and she him. He'd loved her, and she'd loved him. It had been perfect. In that heightened state of love, where nothing could touch them, she saw only a bright and happy future ahead with him. The thought of not being with him had never entered her mind, and yet, when it had happened, it hadn't been as great a wrench as it might have been had she split up with him during a 'normal' time. But then, if her life had been normal, she and Ford would have stayed together, at least, that's what she assumed.

Her parents' passing had made their breakup easier for her to get over. The truth was, she didn't have the mental capacity or the emotional energy to grieve over losing Ford, because the loss of her parents had been insurmountable.

But listening to Ginny speak of her life with Ben didn't seem right at all and it worried her. She watched her sister clear the table, and then load the dishwasher. A familiar heaviness settled in her chest, maybe the type of fear parents experienced when their child was in peril or about to do something terribly wrong.

Nothing Ginny had said about Ben in the last twenty-four hours made Ashleigh feel at ease. This was the man they were supposed to welcome into their lives as a brother-in-law. She didn't know how she would be able to do that.

The day went as well as a Monday could. Ashleigh had a heap of inquiries to deal with, emails and calls that had come in over the weekend from brides anxious about their orders. There were also the dress alterations to deal with from that late showing customer who had interrupted the conversation between her and Ford. That dress was going to need a lot of adjustment. She'd taken the measurements, but she would need to get Eloise to work on this right away, as a matter of priority.

They would manage. Eloise would arrive back home later tonight and Ashleigh would give her these tasks first thing tomorrow. In all the time Eloise had been away, Ashleigh had received one phone call from her when she had landed and then a series of texts, with accompanying photos of her and her group of friends having what looked like a fantastic time.

Later that evening, Ginny made dinner and as the two of them sat and ate quietly, Ashleigh wanted to bring something up but she didn't know what to say or how to say it.

She wasn't sure she wanted to know more about Ben, and at the same time, she needed to step in and say *something*. But each time she looked at her sister, she stopped herself.

Ginny was glowing. With her wheat-blonde hair, shorter than Ashleigh's but similar in color, her skin was sun kissed and her brown eyes glistened.

Ashleigh didn't want to upset her sister by saying anything negative about Ben, but she vowed that she would do so if ever there was another time that Ben upset her.

As Ginny finished clearing up, she announced that Ben was coming to pick her up and they were going out to have dessert.

"You only saw him yesterday. Eloise is coming back later."

"He said we should do date night."

"Date night?" Ashleigh scoffed. He was trying to make it up to Ginny.

"Do you want us to get you anything?" Ginny appeared not to notice Ashleigh's displeasure.

"No thanks."

She decided to wait up for Eloise and sat on the sofa with her laptop in front of her, looking through the online travel guides and putting together some sort of travel itinerary. Recent events had made her even more eager to get away.

A ping on her cell phone caught her attention. It was Eloise texting to tell her that her plane had been delayed due to technical difficulties.

Ashleigh groaned out loud. This was all she needed. She texted her sister.

Ashleigh: **I hope you manage to get back by tomorrow.**

She was about to add that she needed her at work tomorrow, first thing, but decided against it.

Ashleigh: **Going to bed. Have waited up for you long enough.**

Eloise: **Sorry. Meant to text you earlier. We all ended up at a bar. Having fun.**

This was followed by various colorful emojis.

Ended up at a bar. A frown stretched Ashleigh's mouth. Eloise was with her friends and having fun, while she sat here waiting for her like a dodo. She might as well be extinct for all that anyone cared. Her sister hadn't even had the decency to call her and tell her of the delay. She'd texted, and then had the audacity to tell her that she was enjoying herself at the bar.

Frustrated, Ashleigh climbed the stairs and went to bed.

The next morning, she and Ginny were having breakfast when Eloise walked into the house, looking groggy.

"What time do you call this?" Ashleigh asked, sounding more like a mother as she tried to rein in the rude tone. Eloise set her bag to the side, along with her purse, then rubbed her eyes.

"The plane was delayed by so many hours. We didn't set off until after midnight. I'm exhausted." She yawned as if to prove it.

"Good trip?" Ginny asked, biting into her piece of toast.

Eloise perked up at that. "It was amazing!"

"You suddenly don't sound so tired anymore," Ashleigh quipped. "We need to get going," she said to Ginny, and to Eloise, "What time do you think you'll be coming into work?"

"You want me to come in today?"

Ashleigh tensed, the anger building in the base of her stomach and rising slowly upwards. "Do you expect me to give you more time off?"

"I haven't slept," Eloise retorted.

"Why not? You were on a plane."

"Let her sleep for a couple of hours," Ginny pleaded. "She looks a mess."

"Thanks," muttered Eloise. "Let me catch a few hours of sleep and I'll come in."

"It would be a miracle if you did." Ashleigh didn't try to hide the abrasive tone in her voice. She stomped away.

"I heard that!" Eloise cried after her.

"You were supposed to." Ashleigh closed the door behind her. Eloise had some nerve. She had been away since Friday and now she needed more time off to recover from jetlag. How lovely for her. If she worked for a proper employer, instead of in the family business, she'd think twice about asking for time off here, there and everywhere.

Both of her sisters would behave differently if they didn't have the luxury of working in the family business.

With Ginny taking days off all over the place, and now Eloise, Ashleigh resolved to be strict. Otherwise, as experience had taught her, she would be the only one left taking care of everything.

CHAPTER 11

*S*he worked solidly through the morning, checking the time and the door to see when Eloise would show up. The priority for her was to make alterations on that dress for the wedding the weekend after this one and she needed to give it to Eloise the moment she showed up.

When, by noon, there was still no sign of her sister, Ashleigh forced herself to get out to meet Darcie, before she exploded in a fit of rage. She was on her way to the Sunnyside Diner when, walking towards her in the opposite direction, was Ford.

She *felt* him first, more than she saw him. Goosebumps prickled and scampered across her skin. Until she saw that he was with someone, an attractive young woman, and they were both laughing.

It shouldn't have hit like a dart, but it did, seeing him with that pretty young thing. It shouldn't have paralyzed her to the point of making her slow down her walking, but it did.

Ford smiled when her eyes met his, but Ashleigh couldn't smile back. Something twisted deep in her belly, throwing her off course as her eyes bounced between him and the young woman.

"Hey," he said, coming to a stop, and forcing her to do the same, because she'd had no intention of stopping to talk to him.

"Hi." She managed a plastic smile, trying not to let her gaze bounce from the young woman to him.

"This is Maddie, my daughter."

"Oh …." Her voice inflected with hope. She looked from him to the daughter, saw the slight resemblance, in their eyes only, but otherwise there wasn't a trace of Ford in her. "Nice to meet you, Maddie."

"This is Ashleigh," he said, by way of introducing her.

"Nice to meet you," the young girl said, before, "Dad, I'm going to get an ice cream." And off she went, leaving Ashleigh staring at Ford with a sense of relief that puzzled her.

She was over him. Had been so over him. But running into him twice now was making her body react to him in a way that was weirding her out.

"I didn't realize she was all grown up," she said, needing to fill the pregnant pause that he seemed comfortable with. His blue eyes assessed her, making her feel self-conscious of the slight wrinkles around her eyes and mouth. She'd been so frustrated by Eloise this morning that she hadn't checked herself in the mirror before she'd left the house.

"She's eighteen, and going off to college in the fall."

"Eighteen?" She'd assumed she was much younger. An eighteen-year-old daughter suddenly made Ford seem so much older.

"I can't believe it myself. It happens so fast. One minute you're young and free with not a worry in the world, and the next moment your life whizzes by so fast you wonder where the time went." His eyes locked with her so intently, she had to force herself to look away. Something hummed in the space between them, something she couldn't ignore, something that pulled her to him. Not in a physical sense, but an invisible force, so potent that she knew it was real and not a figment of her imagination.

"It happens pretty much like that," she said, agreeing, and wishing he would take his leave. He was blocking her path, and she needed to go.

"You find that, too?"

"Huh?" She had been so busy looking at the slight white hairs that peppered the sides of his face, and the few that were dusted around his hairline to notice much of what he was saying. There was also the broad span of his shoulders, which she didn't remember being as broad before. "Yes. Life happens pretty fast. One minute you're in your twenties, and the next you're staring at fifty."

"You're not fifty. Not even near it," he said, laughing. He appeared to be at ease, while she was still stiff and awkward, trying to fill in the gaps of the twenty years that they had been out of one another's lives. His confident ability to converse with her as if this were normal surprised her.

"I'm not that far from it."

"You don't look a day over thirty, Ash."

Ash.

He was reverting to calling her by the name he'd used when they had been together. And paying her compliments as well. She felt light and flirty, enjoying it, and tucked her hair behind her ear, resisting the urge to smooth it down and make it tidy.

"Well, I am."

"Not working today?" he asked.

"I'm always working." She sighed, perhaps a little too loudly.

"Yeah?" There was a wealth of questioning behind that 'yeah.' Ford could read her better than anyone she knew. "Busy day?"

"It's always busy, and Mondays are one of our busiest days." There were lots of inquiries to deal with that had come in over the weekend.

"You've always held everything together, Ash."

She wanted to tell him not to call her Ash, and not to talk about time whizzing by. For them especially, time and the past were topics to be avoided, and yet here he was, openly discussing them. She didn't want to be reminded of the past and what might have been, but even though she didn't want this conversation, it felt easy. She missed that knowingness that he had for her. Nobody else had ever understood her as well as Ford did. He'd been the one to console her after her parents' accident. He'd been the one to hold her tight, to wipe away her tears and to comfort her.

Goodness, she'd missed him, she only realized that now, having closed off her mind to him as soon as she'd found out he'd fallen in love with someone else. It hadn't hurt then, as much as it could have, should have. Breaking up with him, telling him that it wasn't going to work, that she was never going to leave Whisper Falls, and that he would be making a mistake if he came back here, had hurt more.

But him walking back into her life and being so familiar, so friendly again, after such a long time of not having any access to him, it was like a time jump. She'd gone back to being that twenty-one-year-old again with him, and it was dangerous.

"Someone had to," she replied then, because she didn't want to dwell on that part of their history. "Why are you back here?" she asked, though it came out harsher than she intended.

"You sound like you'd rather I wasn't." He seemed to sense her frostiness.

"I didn't mean it like that."

"I'm taking some time away. Thinking things over, and my mom isn't well. I want to spend some time with her, more time than I have in the past. I want that for Maddie as well."

"It must be different being back, after living in a big city."

He tilted his head. "It is, but in a good way. I'm not a city dweller. I'm a native from these parts."

"It must have been amazing in Boston."

His face turned serious then. "I wish … I wish you'd had a chance to come."

She looked away, feeling uncomfortable that he was bringing back old memories, especially about Boston. "Things happen. I'm fine here."

"I'm not sure about Boston."

"No?" She couldn't believe that he was opening up to her like this.

"There's nothing for me in Boston. Maddie is going to college in the fall, and my mom is getting old. I would rather be here to take care of her."

"It makes sense, I suppose."

"We should get together, Ash."

"Whatever for?" She tucked her hair behind her ear again, her stomach fluttery as if she'd tickled it with a feather. Drawn into this spell with him again, she couldn't help but remember the young man he used to be, and the young couple they had been before their lives and dreams had been shattered, forcing them to go off in different directions. Was it possible to reconnect again now? Was he being polite, as an old boyfriend, or was he looking for something more? Did he think of that old life, the one she had denied him, with her?

But, more importantly, did *she* want any of that?

"Whatever for?" He laughed, his eyes crinkling at the corners. "To catch up on old times, you, me and Darcie. I saw her a few days ago."

Oh. He wanted to connect with the three of them. Here she was flying ahead with a whole heap of romantic notions and he only wanted to connect with his old friends.

Silly, deluded woman that she was.

"We should, sometime," she agreed, feeling the pressure slide away. Just the two of them meeting seemed like too much. With Darcie in the mix, it would be okay. "I have to go. I'm meeting someone for lunch." She could have told him it was Darcie, but she wanted to keep it vague, and hoped he would wonder who it might be.

CHAPTER 12

*H*e walked over to where Maddie was waiting for him.

"Who was she?" his daughter asked, licking her ice cream cone. They started to walk again. He wanted to show her more of the town, and the people and places he had grown up with truly felt like coming home. It was comforting and slow-paced, the life back here. He had missed that and he wished he had visited more often. He would have had it not been for his wife, now his ex-wife. Susan hadn't liked the small-town feel, though Whisper Falls wasn't such a small town that everyone knew everyone else's business. It was also affluent and upscale, with boutique shops and a busy town center.

It wasn't that he'd hated Boston. Quite the opposite. He had loved its vibrancy when he'd first moved there, and securing a well-paid job had given him a nice start. Working for his uncle had paid off, and after many years, he had gone on to start his own small practice, and had done well enough from it to be able to afford a decent house.

Boston was expensive. It had helped that Susan was a doctor at the local hospital, working crazy hours. But her long hours and dedication to her career, along with his to his business, had caused problems between them. These had been manageable at first, but as Maddie grew older, and as time wore on, he and Susan started to drift apart. The pressure of work meant that they barely had time for one another, and the real problems had started when they had ended up having separate bedrooms.

It hadn't been intentional at first. Their marriage had been good, and they had loved fiercely. Susan had been the perfect wife and mother, but when she had suggested they have separate bedrooms, because she worked odd hours sometimes and didn't want to disturb him, it was then that the chinks in their carefully constructed life started to appear.

Over the years, during the few times he'd returned to Whisper Falls, he'd heard what Ashleigh was up to. It was easy because she and her sisters ran the bridal shop which was a draw to the town. There was that time some years ago when his father had died and he'd run into her in town. Ashleigh had come over to him. It had been an odd encounter. He was still reeling from the pain of losing his father but talking to her for the first time since they had broken up had been surreal. He'd been so numb that he hadn't been able to process it.

But this time it all felt different, returning to Whisper Falls. He hadn't come back because his marriage had broken down. Thankfully, he and Susan had parted amicably, and nobody else was involved. He had returned to take care of his mom, but also because he wanted a break and to be among people he had grown up with, and to revisit the places of his youth.

But seeing the woman who had once upon a time captivated his heart—a woman who looked the same now as she did then, a woman he had never forgotten, because the tragedy that had befallen her family had haunted him—it had rekindled something from his past.

When Ashleigh spoke and stared into his eyes, she took him

back to that carefree time and place where they had been when they were young and ready to start their lives, standing on the precipice of a great adventure. Only it wasn't meant to be.

He sometimes wondered how things would have been had tragedy not hit Ashleigh's life; if they had traveled around Europe as they had planned, and if she'd studied for her journalism degree.

If they had been together …

This thought had started floating around the edges of his mind when he had first seen her walking in the town with Darcie. He couldn't help but go visit her at the shop later, because he felt compelled to.

There was no guilt now, no reason he could not dream, because he was single again. He hadn't come looking for Ashleigh Rose, but having bumped into her, he couldn't help but be drawn into the old memories.

The question was, did she feel the same way, or was she with someone?

CHAPTER 13

*D*arcie was already sitting and waiting for her at one of the red and white gingham flocked tables.

"Where have you been? I've been waiting for ages!" Darcie's menu was closed, but Ashleigh's was laid out ready for her to decide.

"I got held up." She sat down, glanced quickly through the menu. "I know what I'm having."

"We don't have long. I have to get back." Darcie said. "I'm sorry we couldn't meet yesterday."

"Don't worry."

"Everything okay?"

Ashleigh opened the menu then closed it, because she knew what she wanted. The usual. "Ginny's having a few wobbles. Nothing major," she lied. "Let's order quickly."

Having summoned the server and quickly placed their orders, she recounted the recent encounter with Ford.

"You saw him just now?"

"Just now. He was with his daughter." Ashleigh sat back in her chair, feeling her heart rate start to slow down. "It's almost as if he's following me around." When Darcie's eyes widened, she told her about that first time when he had come to the shop. "He said he was passing by, but you don't pass by the shop. You come there for a reason."

Darcie's grin stretched out her mouth. "And he obviously did. He wanted to say hello."

Ashleigh made a face.

"Why is that such a problem?" Darcie asked.

"Because …"

"He's divorced." Darcie's eyebrow lifted, her smile turned mischievous.

"He said we should meet up."

Darcie's smile widened even more.

"He said for the *three* of us to meet up," Ashleigh clarified.

"That would be nice. Would be nice for the two of you to catch up too." Darcie had known them both since high school and knew of their history. She also had a sharp memory and probably hadn't forgotten how heartbroken Ashleigh had been when she had split up with him.

"The two of us? Don't even go there. Whatever you're thinking, don't."

"What am I thinking?" Darcie jerked her head.

"You know."

Darcie shrugged. "I'm thinking he's a handsome unattached guy, and he's not going to remain unattached for long."

Ashleigh groaned. "I have plans."

"He might not be looking to get back with you, Ash. Maybe now that he's divorced, he just wants to see how you are, because he can, because his wife isn't around."

"Ford coming back doesn't change a thing for me." Of that Ashleigh was adamant.

Their food arrived and she glanced at her watch. She prayed that Eloise would be at the shop when she returned, because there was a lot to bring her up to date on, and they had to run through the plans for Ginny's bachelorette party.

"We're organizing Ginny's bachelorette party," she announced, not wanting to talk about Ford. Her feelings were all muddled up inside and she needed time to sift through them properly. She wasn't ready for a Darcie-inspection just yet.

"What fun! She doesn't have long to go, does she?"

"No." Ashleigh fell silent, thinking about her sister. Ginny and Ben were always on her mind lately, and she desperately needed to tell Eloise.

"You said she had the wobbles." Darcie had picked up on it. Ashleigh looked up and sighed, then told her what had happened and why she hadn't been able to meet her for brunch.

"I don't know what to say," said Darcie, picking up an onion ring and taking a bite. "Poor Ginny. Is she okay?"

"She's in love, she thinks he walks on water. She can't see his glaring faults."

"Maybe he'll change when they're married."

Ashleigh looked at her, and they both knew the truth. Men didn't change. People didn't change; not unless something in their lives was causing them so much pain that they had no choice but to.

Ben's life was pretty fine. He had done well to end up with someone like Ginny, and he knew it. And until Ginny toughened up and called him out for his behavior, he was going to continue behaving the way he had. Like a douchebag.

"Uh," Ashleigh skewered a slice of cucumber on her fork. "I don't want to talk about Ben. It depresses me, and makes me angry at the same time."

"Great. Tell me more about Ford."

"I just did."

"But tell me again what he said, and what he told you, and what his plans are."

For some reason, it was easier to talk about Ford.

When she later returned to work, she had never been happier to see the sight of Eloise's back.

"You're here," said Ashleigh, stating the obvious.

"That was a long lunch. I thought you'd left for the day," Eloise returned. Ashleigh stared at her with a blank expression, trying to determine if her sister was joking or being deadly serious.

"You're complaining about my lunch?"

"I'm joking," said Eloise. She had the book of orders in her hand and open wide. "What's this?" she tapped a pen on the entry Ashleigh had scribbled down for the woman who'd shown up late on Saturday.

Ashleigh explained what had happened, and that the woman was in a panic because her wedding day wasn't far away.

"I told her we'd fix it, so you have to as a matter of priority. That's why I needed you here first thing in the morning."

"I'm here now, aren't I?"

"Take a look at her measurements. They're in the folder. Her dress is in the back. She's coming to pick it up this weekend."

"I'm on it." Eloise disappeared in the back. Ashleigh followed her, having looked around to see that Ginny was on the shop floor.

"I'm on it," Eloise repeated, walking over to the sewing area in one corner of the office. The dress was hanging up in its garment bag. Ashleigh glanced over her shoulder to make sure that they were alone.

"Ginny came home upset this weekend, after shopping."

Eloise opened the folder for alterations and started looking through it, searching for the notes of the alterations that needed doing. "Upset about what?"

"She and Ben had an argument over some things they were looking at for the house."

Eloise looked up at her. "What did they argue about?"

"A lamp. She liked it and he didn't. He said a few things, and Ginny got upset—you know how fragile she is at the moment. She came home in tears."

"They fought over a lamp?"

"Over a lamp."

"That man." Eloise's face hardened, her eyes narrowed. "What do we do?" she asked, as if this were a problem they could easily fix.

"We pray. He came over a few hours later and apologized and they've made up."

"It's always that easy with Ginny."

They were both quiet for a while.

"He'd … he'd better not hurt her," said Eloise finally.

"I think he already has, emotionally, but she falls for his lines and they make up again. We can't do anything. We tried to warn her, but she's in love, and love is blind."

"So, we stand by and let him do it again?" asked Eloise.

"We support her as best as we can, and pray that it won't happen again, and that he'll grow up. Ginny is too soft, and she needs to stand up to him."

"Or not get married," Eloise offered, getting out a tape measure.

"It's too late for that."

"Speaking of that, I know what Ginny wants to do on her bachelorette party. I've made all the arrangements."

Ashleigh's brow puckered. Eloise had done all of this without consulting her? That was a first. "Great."

"I figured you were angry about me jetting off to Las Vegas, so I took care of everything while I was in Vegas."

"Do you want me to clap?" Ashleigh asked, rolling her eyes.

"It would be nice," Eloise tossed back. "Anyway," she opened the sewing basket and got out a needle and thread. "We're spending the day at The Connington. She's staying there the night with her friends, and we're not."

"Are we too old for her and her friends?"

"You might be." Eloise smiled. "But we are all spending the day in the pool, and the Jacuzzi, and the hot tub, and we've all got two beauty treatments each. Obviously, her friends can have more if they want. I've arranged food, nibbles and snacks and drinks during the day, and then we're having dinner there in the evening. And after that, you and I are coming home."

"We'll have to make sure everything is taken care of in the shop." Ashleigh wondered if one of them needed to stay back and keep an eye on the business. Spring was a busy time and they couldn't afford to mess up any bride's wedding day.

"Oh, no, you don't." Eloise waggled her finger at her. "You're coming along. We are not going to miss this."

"You've already been on a party weekend. Maybe you could stay back?" Ashleigh suggested, as a joke.

"I'm always ready for a party."

"Don't we know it."

"It will be fine. We'll get all the assistants to come in."

It would be fine. She had to remember to not be so hands-on or worried about every little aspect of the business. How would she ever manage being away for months if she couldn't stop worrying about things? She turned to go. "You haven't told me what you did in Vegas."

"We had a lot of fun, let's just leave it at that."

Ashleigh nodded and walked away, wondering just how old Eloise seemed to think she was.

CHAPTER 14

Surprisingly, given recent events, the week passed peacefully enough. Ashleigh was relieved to find that Ginny was upbeat and as happy as ever, and there didn't seem to be any further arguments between her and Ben. Eloise had made the relevant alterations on all the dresses that had needed them, and things were moving on just fine.

Every so often, Ashleigh would wonder if now was the time to drop a hint about her future plans. This particular morning, when the three of them were at the shop together before they had opened it to customers, seemed like the perfect time. But the arrival of a van outside halted any such thing.

Another wedding dress had been delivered. Eloise opened the door to receive it, until she cried out that it was Ginny's wedding dress, because it was addressed to her by name, and not The Bridal Shop.

In a rush of excitement, they all crowded around as Eloise carried the huge garment carrier to the changing room.

"Let me! Let me!" Ginny cried, eager to be the first one to open it and take a look. She let out a gasp, which was then echoed by Eloise and Ashleigh as Ginny slowly and carefully took out her wedding dress. They helped her to get all of it out of the carrier so that it wouldn't snag anywhere.

It was a gorgeous white silk wedding dress, with a bateau neckline that framed the shoulders, and sleeves that were made of floral lace. The dress flared out from the waist, in soft folds cushioned by an underskirt in triple silk organza. The back was cut low, not too low, but low enough, and there was a tiny column of buttons going all the way down; shiny satin buttons, just like Ginny had wanted. She and Eloise had given into her demands and surprised her. The buttons added a pretty little level of detail, and the whole ensemble was jawdroppingly stunning.

"Try it on then," urged Eloise. They carefully helped her carry it into the fitting room, then waited outside when Ginny shooed them away.

"I need help with the buttons." Ginny stuck her neck around the red velvet curtain, her face a picture of pure joy. Eloise squealed in excitement. "You look beautiful, oh, my goodness, she looks so beautiful!" And then disappeared into the changing room.

Ashleigh's heart thumped with excitement, and when Ginny stepped out, the air punched right out of her lungs. Her mouth fell open.

"You look ... you look ..." She couldn't get the words out and her eyes welled up in tears.

"You look like a princess," Eloise gushed. Her eyes were also filled with tears. Ginny looked from one to the other. "You two!" She gave a dismissive wave of her hand, as she made her way, barefoot, towards the large mirror outside the fitting room area. When she saw her reflection, she almost stumbled back, hand on heart.

"Told you that you looked amazing," said Ashleigh, sniffling as the tears threatened to fall from her eyes. She wished her parents were here, and she felt a deep ache in her heart that they would never see Ginny. She missed them more than anything right at this very moment.

"Ginny, you look so beautiful. *Sooo* beautiful!" She clasped her hands together.

"Doesn't she just?" Eloise whispered. The two of them gaped at her, speechless and utterly transfixed. Even in her bare feet and with no makeup on, and with her hair hanging loose over her shoulders, Ginny looked ethereal.

"I wish Mom and Dad were here," she said, her voice shaky with emotion.

"Don't … you'll get me started," Eloise clutched a hand to her chest.

But it was too late. The tears fell, thick and fast, down Ginny's cheeks, and Ashleigh could hold it back no more. Soon, the three of them were crying, silent tears, a bittersweet mixture of sadness and joy.

CHAPTER 15

Their beds and dressers were being delivered to the new house. Ginny waited for the deliverymen, along with Ben, to move everything into the house, and when they left, she stared at the furniture, a feeling of joy bursting from her heart.

Everything was coming together perfectly.

Their home.

The painting was finished, and the smell of fresh paint lingered in the air and she had opened the windows to help get rid of it. She stepped back and admired how well the white dresser looked in what would be their master bedroom. It would go well with the curtains and bed linen they had chosen.

Ben had half put up the curtains when the deliverymen had arrived, and now he was back up on the ladder, putting up the rest of them. She pulled away the plastic wrapping on the mattress, letting it air for a while before she put the linen on it.

They were going to spend their first night here, before leaving for their honeymoon in Montana. Two weeks in Montana with Ben. She couldn't wait. Eloise had booked everything for her bachelorette party and had notified her friends about the time schedule and what they had planned.

She watched Ben finish putting up the second curtain and sighed with delight as he came over to her and took her hand. "They look gorgeous."

The green curtains with a block pattern in black and gray brought a splash of color to the room. Ben had been right. She'd wanted color on the walls, maybe a hint of pale blue, or pale green, but he had been right. White did make the room look bigger, and it was fresh and airy, and the curtains popped.

She fetched the bed linen which she had washed, dried and ironed even though it was all new. She wanted it soft and smelling fresh.

Ben started to help her as she started to put the covers on the pillows. "Eloise has organized my bachelorette party," she announced.

"Cool. What are you doing?"

She told him about the plans for her friends and sisters to go to The Connington, and told him of the things they had planned. "And then we're all having dinner together in the evening, but my sisters are going home and me and my friends are staying the night there."

"And then?"

"And then we'll probably stay up all night talking and stuff."

"Is that all?"

"It's what I want to do," she replied. Eloise was the wildest of the three of them. If her sister had had her own way, Ginny was sure there would be a few racy things involved, like some adult games and drinking games, but Ginny didn't care for such things. She hadn't dared ask Eloise what she and her friends had done in Las Vegas.

"Don't you want to do something crazy for the last time?" asked Ben, throwing a pillow with its new cover up against the headrest.

"Like what?" Anxiety spiked in her chest.

"I don't know. Like maybe go dancing, and see some strippers?"

She made a face. "Why would I want to do something like that?"

He snorted. "It's what women do."

"Some women, maybe. Not me."

"Tyler's planned my bachelor party."

Her insides froze. Tyler was a bad influence on him and she didn't like the sound of this. "What are you guys doing?"

"We're going to Cooper's."

She dropped the pillow case she had been holding. "Cooper's?"

He nodded, smiling as he picked up the pillow case and reached for the pillow she'd been holding.

"But, Cooper's … it's …" It was a bar out of town, *way* out of town, and the only reason she knew about it was because he'd told her about that time when one of his friends was getting married and his bachelor party had involved a trip to Cooper's. Ben hadn't left out any of the details of that event which was why Ginny knew about the bar in which inappropriately dressed women served drinks to men and were given huge tips. It was loud and raucous, judging from what Ben had said. "Why are you going there?"

"Because I want one night of crazy with my friends."

One night of crazy. Nausea rolled in her stomach. Her dreams adrift on a choppy sea.

"Awww, babe, no," he whined. "Tell me you're not going to have a problem with this."

"You're going to a bar to drink all night and look at women who are almost naked, and you're wondering why I have a problem with that?"

"It's what men do, Ginny. Stop being such a prude." He started to put the bedspread on the bed, but she flinched at the idea of sharing this bed with him knowing that he had every intention of visiting that awful place.

He put his arm around her shoulder and hugged her to his chest. "Why are you so worried, Ginny? I love you. Only you. It's all harmless fun, babe. Stop worrying."

She bit her lower lip. The idea of Ben in a place like that skewered her heart.

"Hey," he lifted her chin with his finger. "I. Love. You." And then he kissed her, but her toes didn't curl, and she was reluctant to put her arms around him. "Hey," he said, pulling away. "If it's going to make you that miserable, then I won't go." He threw his hands in the air, and she knew he would be sullen for the rest of the day.

"Fine then. Go, but just … be careful. Stay away from Tyler."

"It's harmless fun, babe. Don't you worry."

CHAPTER 16

"But I came here last weekend, and your sister took the measurements. How can they be so wrong?"

Ashleigh stepped out of the office and was making her way to the counter when she overheard the commotion in the area outside the changing rooms. She recognized the woman whose measurements she had taken and her heart lurched. Had she messed something up?

"Don't worry. We can fix this. It's not a problem at all." Eloise tried to reassure her.

"I'm getting married next weekend!" the woman wailed. "I don't have time to keep coming here. You were recommended to me by a friend who spoke highly of you, but you can't even get the measurements right. What a mess!"

Ashleigh stepped in. "What's wrong?"

"It's tight under my ribs."

"I took it in according to your measurements," Eloise muttered under her breath.

She had messed up. Ashleigh cleared her throat. "I'm sorry. It's my fault." She completely understood the woman's anger and frustration. "I made a mistake with the measurements. How about we take ten percent off the price for you, and I'll arrange to have this delivered to you by courier as soon as it's fixed?"

"What if it doesn't fit again?"

"Unless your weight fluctuates again, which I think is highly unlikely within the next few days, I don't think we'll have to worry about that." Eloise flashed a smile at the woman.

"I am not risking it. This is a disaster! I'm getting married next Saturday. Next Saturday."

I'm trying my best, lady. Ashleigh took a few deep breaths in. That weekend when Eloise had been away had been hectic. And then Ford had walked in, to make matters worse, and she hadn't been able to focus. "I can do better than that, seeing that it was my fault. We'll have this fixed for you by tomorrow, and you can come in tomorrow—or we'll arrange to have the dress delivered to you—tomorrow."

"Tomorrow?" Eloise asked, giving her a we-don't-open-on-Sunday look.

Ashleigh had made up her mind. "We don't open on Sunday, but we will on this occasion." It was the least she could do. Their reputation was everything, this was how word spread about their business. She couldn't afford to let her lack of focus give rise to bad publicity.

"You'll do that? For me?" The customer looked startled.

"Of course we will." Ashleigh turned to her sister. "Could you take more measurements, please?" She looked away, not wanting to stare at Eloise's stone-cold expression. The customer seemed immediately at ease.

"I'll leave you in my capable sister's hands," Ashleigh told her, and walked over to the counter leaving Eloise to deal with the distraught bride. Eloise would never get any measurement wrong. This was her area of expertise. While it wasn't Ashleigh's, she could take measurements and she was surprised that she had messed up as badly as she did. Ford showing up at the end of the day had made her all flustered.

"We're going to open on Sunday? Thanks." Eloise sniped as she later walked into the office and hovered around Ashleigh's desk.

"The woman was distraught. What else could I do?"

"Why were the measurements so off? You never get them wrong."

Ashleigh threw her sister a hard glare. Eloise folded her arms.

"I'm not making a dig at you. It's just that you never make mistakes like that."

"Maybe it was the fact that you and Ginny were off that day and I was overwhelmed, having worked Friday alone –"

"You had the assistants."

"But they don't take care of all the things we do."

"But to get them so wrong, Ash? The woman could hardly breathe."

Ashleigh's mouth twisted and she struggled to compose herself. "Maybe I was tired and worn out. I'm allowed to make some mistakes."

Eloise groaned loudly. "That's not what I'm saying. Don't go getting all preachy with me."

"Preachy? I'm only stating a fact. You're the one who jetted off to Vegas. And then Ginny and Ben argued, and Ginny came home crying, and I had to pick up the pieces of that fallout."

"You said that happened the next day."

"I'm saying that I have a lot of things to deal with. It all adds up." *I need time away too.*

"I'm sorry you have to play mom more than you should."

"I'm not mom. Mom's irreplaceable." She fought to keep back the sob which was in her throat. She didn't tear up anymore when they talked about their parents. They had been alone for so long now, that memories of their mother and father were precious pieces of nostalgia, taken out like a valuable piece of art that was admired when attention was drawn to it, but then put away for another time. Something that was cherished forever in their hearts, if not always in plain sight.

"I'm sorry. That was below the belt. I didn't mean to say that. You're the best sister we could have. I'm sorry." Eloise's eyes teared up. Ashleigh narrowed her eyes because Eloise didn't resort to crying so easily.

"What's the matter with you?"

"Nothing."

"It can't be nothing when your eyes are leaking."

They both laughed at this. A childhood reminder of what Ginny used to say as a child, in the early years after their parents' passing, when she and Eloise seemed to cry almost daily.

"Is anyone going to help me?" Ginny popped her head around the corner, and luckily Eloise had her back to her. Typical, thought Ashleigh. Alone on the shop floor for a few moments and Ginny couldn't cope.

"We'll be out," she and Eloise said in unison.

"Ford came into the shop," Ashleigh announced. She might as well mention it to Eloise.

"Ford?"

"Ford. He came here that day, when I had to take the measurements. I was all over the place."

Eloise pulled her chair over and sat down, as if the shock of this news needed that kind of response. "He was *here?* Who's getting married?"

Ashleigh nodded. "Nobody. He's back in town, and he's divorced."

"He came here to tell you that?"

"Not that, as such. He said he just wanted to see how I was, and what I was up to."

"Why didn't you tell me before?" Eloise demanded.

"I'm telling you now."

"We used to talk more, before…" Eloise's eyes turned glassy, as if she felt sad. "We've just become so …"

"Jaded?" Ashleigh offered. Living together, and working together, spending all this time together, they had started to get on top of one another. Running the family business had become all-consuming.

"Maybe," Eloise replied.

"Are you going to come help me or not?" Ginny's angry face stared at them both. "It's getting crazy busy out here."

Eloise got up. "I'll go." She walked over to the door then turned around. "We'll have to talk later. I want to know every little thing he said to you."

Ashleigh tucked her hair behind her ears, and stifled a little yawn. "It wasn't anything significant."

"But it was enough to get you all worked up and get the measurements wrong." Eloise winked at her and left.

CHAPTER 17

*T*hey'd been talking about Ginny's bachelorette party when Ginny had walked into the kitchen looking a little subdued. When they'd asked her what was wrong, she'd said she was tired from getting things situated at their new house, and hadn't elaborated.

She and Eloise looked at one another, a worried expression on both their faces. Ashleigh opened her mouth to say something but the look on Eloise's face warned her against it.

Eloise didn't like confrontation, but Ashleigh worried and wanted to get to the bottom of things. At times like this, she wondered what their mother and father would have done had they been around.

They ate breakfast, with only her and Eloise talking about having to go into the shop because of one customer. But then Ben had called, and Ginny had lit up like a firecracker, rushing to eat her breakfast. She announced that Ben was picking her up again, and a few minutes later she left, before they'd even finished their breakfast.

"Am I overthinking things or was she quiet when she came downstairs? One phone call from Ben and she's all happy again."

"You can't read things into everything," Eloise told her. "Ginny just woke up. She's not always with it first thing in the morning."

"I wasn't sure if they'd had another argument."

"Did it seem as if they had? She couldn't get out of here fast enough the moment he called her."

"True." Ashleigh clasped her hands around her cup of coffee and groaned. "I don't want to go into work today. I want to be in the backyard doing my sun salutations."

Eloise got up. "You don't have to be there. I've taken care of it. I have a little bit of sewing left to do and I'll have it done by the time the customer gets there." They'd already agreed on a time that was convenient for the client. Any time before noon. Eloise had been working on the dress yesterday, making sure that it would fit exactly right.

"How did she lose so much weight so fast?" Ashleigh asked.

"She went on a diet."

"She didn't look as if she needed to." She remembered the woman from the first time she'd come into the shop, a few months ago. She looked perfectly fine. Voluptuous, was the word Ashleigh would have used to describe her. She wished she had that type of lush and fuller figure, like Ginny did.

"You know how it is. Women want to look their utmost best."

"Losing that much weight that fast isn't the utmost best, I'd say."

"You don't have a weight problem," Eloise remarked.

"Neither did she, as far as I could see." Ashleigh got up slowly. "I'll come with you."

"Why? I told you I can take care of it."

"I made the mistake in the first place; I should be there to make sure the customer is completely happy."

Eloise placed her hands on her hips. "Don't you trust me?"

"Of course I do!" This wasn't about trust; it was about her

needing to ensure that everything was one hundred percent to the customer's satisfaction.

"You can't let go, that's your problem." Eloise picked up her breakfast dishes and walked over to the sink. "And another problem? You think Ginny and I are less capable than you."

"That's not true." She didn't understand why Eloise was getting so defensive.

"Then why do you need to be there? I've told you I can take care of it. I can handle this customer. I'm the one who's made the alterations, not you, and frankly, I don't need you overseeing my work and having the last word. I can ensure everything is to the customer's satisfaction. Quit treating us like little children, Ash."

This was what Eloise thought? Ashleigh stepped back until her back was against the countertop. She hadn't seen this coming. "I don't treat you like little children."

"You want to micromanage both of us."

"That's not true."

"Then why did you feel the need to come to the shop today?"

Ashleigh didn't have an answer for that.

"You're always complaining that Ginny and I go off and do our own things, and you're always mad when you're the only one at work, but have you ever thought that it's not our fault? It's yours. If you had a life, you'd have things to do, instead of getting all temperamental when we want to go do things. I'm going now, and I'd prefer it if you didn't feel the need to oversee me every step of the way."

Her sister stormed out before Ashleigh could say a word. "Have a life? I do have a life," she mumbled to herself, smarting over her sister's comments.

She did have a life. Of course she did.

.   .   .

A short while later, she met with Darcie, making up for the brunch they'd missed the last time. "She thinks I treat them like children, and all because I want to do my job properly."

"And what does your job entail?"

"You know what my job is." They walked along.

"But what do *you* think your job is?"

"Taking care of things at the shop, dealing with brides, helping them to find their perfect dresses. Making sure that this is 'where dreams begin,'" she said, mimicking the last words in an exaggerated way.

"But who took the measurements this time?"

"Eloise."

"Who did the alterations?" Darcie asked.

"Eloise."

"And how old is she?"

"Thirty-five, no thirty-six."

"Then why did you feel the need to be there?"

Ashleigh considered her reply carefully. Darcie made her feel as if she were in a trial situation in the courtroom. She felt she was being tricked into making a confession of some sort. Or having a realization. "Because ... because ..." She had no answer.

"Isn't this nicer? You and me out walking on this beautiful sunny day?"

"Yes." It sure did beat being stuck in the shop all day. Eloise was right. She didn't have to be there today. Eloise could handle it alone. "Am I controlling?"

"Do you want me to answer that?"

Ashleigh groaned. She'd considered herself as a consummate professional, running the business as best as she could and offering the highest level of service. In the process, she'd installed herself as the main owner, over and above her sisters. When Aunt Becky had taught her the ropes, she'd seen herself as the main person in charge, along with her aunt. As her sisters grew older and came on-board, she should have seen them as worthy contemporaries, but she hadn't.

Darcie threw her arm around her shoulder. "You're not too controlling, Ash. You just want to provide the best level of service, and you're attached to your business in a way that maybe Eloise and Ginny aren't. But you have to ask yourself, how are you ever going to leave them to run it, if you can't let Eloise take care of a bride who was having a hissy fit?"

"It wasn't a hissy fit. She was right to be so angry. I did mess up with her measurements."

"The power of Ford over you."

It took a minute for the words to make sense, and then she slapped her friend's arm playfully. "That is not true."

"Have you managed to find out yet why he's divorced?"

"No! I wouldn't even dream of asking him."

"Then I'll ask him."

"What? Why?"

"Ford!" Darcie yelled.

"What are you doing?" she hissed, not daring to turn and stare. Ford was nearby and it made her heart thump even louder.

"Ford!" Darcie ignored her and was waving like a madwoman. She saw him up ahead of them. He had his back turned, but she could make out that tall broad-shouldered frame of his anywhere.

He slowly turned around, a casual grin decorating his face as he appeared to wait for them.

"Come on," Darcie hooked her arm into hers and started speed-walking towards him.

"What are you doing?" Ashleigh cried in a low angry voice. She did not want to be frog-marched to Ford of all people.

"Hey." Darcie's voice boomed with exuberance.

"Hi." His eyes twinkled as he acknowledged them both. Was it her imagination or did his gaze linger over her for longer?

Boom-boom-boom went her heart.

"Hey, Ford."

"What are you doing in town?" Darcie asked, the familiar tone and manner of her speaking surprising Ashleigh.

"I was going for a walk, and then meeting a friend."

"Huh." Darcie turned to her. "He was going for a walk too."

"And meeting a friend," I reminded her. Their eyes locked, and she wondered what friend and where?

"We're getting something to eat at the diner. Care to join us?"

"I would love to—"

"But he's meeting a friend," Ashleigh said. Ford's eyes locked onto hers and they stared at one another for a few seconds longer than was necessary, the aftereffect of his gaze making her cheeks color.

"That's right. I am meeting a friend, but if I wasn't, I would have loved to join you both."

"That's a shame, never mind." Ashleigh turned to leave but Darcie's arm in hers prevented her, and Darcie wasn't moving.

"Another time, hopefully," he said.

"That's a shame. A real, crying shame." Darcie stared at him while Ashleigh forced herself to look at the shops on the other side of the street. Anywhere but at Ford walking away from them.

"He is a fine figure of a man," her friend continued.

"You sound like the Ford Montgomery Appreciation Society," Ashleigh snapped. "Let me remind you that you're married."

"I'm happily married," Darcie shot back. "But it would be a crying shame, a *real* crying shame to let a man like that get away from you for the second time."

"Enough!" Ashleigh pulled her arm out of Darcie's hold and faced her. "Will. You. Stop. Trying to force that man into my arms. We aren't together. We won't be together. There is no together."

"That's the most animated I've seen you in weeks," declared Darcie, not at all bothered by her words or tone.

"I'm starving. I need to eat," growled Ashleigh and stormed into the diner.

CHAPTER 18

*E*loise's alterations had worked perfectly, and the customer had been over the moon. She'd also been taken aback that they had opened the store just for her. Everything had worked out fine.

The next few weeks sailed along smoothly. Ginny was always in a cheery mood, leading Ashleigh to think that perhaps she was the one who was making a lot out of their squabbles.

A new house and a wedding were enough to make couples bicker. She was the one at fault for making so much out of something that was probably so normal.

With things being on an even keel, she'd made up her mind to let Eloise know of her travel plans before she told Ginny. She planned to tell her when they came back from celebrating Ginny's bachelorette party.

With this on the horizon, she found herself thinking more of her great escape. It wasn't the way she wanted to label her trip, but great escape seemed like the perfect term, and she felt guilty for thinking of life at the shop, and with her sisters, as something she needed to escape from.

Maybe she felt this way because she was the only one who

hadn't left for too long, because of a sense of duty and responsibility. But Ginny would be gone soon, and she would have her own life. Eloise was right, they hadn't considered what might happen if Ginny started a family and no longer wanted to work. They would have to get more help, and somehow run the business between the two of them.

And what if Ashleigh herself wasn't so eager to return to her previous life after her vacation? What if she didn't return at all? It was a far-fetched notion, but not completely impossible. A taste of freedom might give her other ideas.

But what then of the business her mother had so lovingly started and probably wanted to run on for future generations? They would have to think of something. Maybe Eloise would surprise them all and keep it running?

Ashleigh didn't want to dwell on reasons which might fill her with guilt and make her stay. The age of fifty was seven years away, but life seemed to have gotten faster with each passing year. She'd be fifty soon enough, in the blink of an eye, and she could already feel it creeping up on her. This might be her one chance to make a break for good.

But it wasn't only her plans for the future that had her thinking a lot in her quiet times. There was also the question of Ford.

He hadn't been in her mind for a long time, until he'd suddenly reappeared in her life. Now she couldn't stop thinking about him and she wasn't sure how she felt about that.

CHAPTER 19

*S*he could do this. Spend an entire day at The Connington, leaving the assistants in charge of the shop, and maybe, if she could relax enough, she could enjoy herself.

Ginny was the happiest that they had seen in a while, and Eloise had started the bachelorette weekend with prosecco for breakfast.

Once at the hotel, they barely saw Ginny who looked to be having a lot of fun with her friends. Eloise and Ashleigh knew some of them, others were names that Ginny had mentioned in passing. They joined in, but kept a slight distance, leaving Ginny and her friends to enjoy the day.

Eloise had confiscated Ashleigh's cell phone so that she couldn't even call the shop to check that everything was running smoothly.

They spent the morning alternating between sitting in the Jacuzzi, enjoying the steam room, as well as having beauty treatments. They also had the use of the pool.

There was brunch, snacks and nibbles throughout the day, with a dinner in the evening.

It was a day of fun and joy, and at dinnertime, Ashleigh made a toast to her sister, and Eloise added to it, saying that they wished their sister the happiest of times. Ginny beamed with joy and everyone clapped and raised their glasses. But the most touching and memorable highlight of the evening was when Ginny got up and made a short speech, telling her friends that she was the luckiest girl in the world to have the best sisters. She had turned glassy-eyed when talking about her mom and dad, and she wished that they, too, had been here.

"I know nothing will bring them back, but I have been blessed with sisters who cared for me just like my parents would have. It must have been hard for them, to have a sister they had to parent, but I want to thank them both from the bottom of my heart for always being here for me, and for always having my back, and to my sister Ashleigh, who takes care of both of us, I love you so much more than words can ever say. To my sister Eloise, who is my partner in crime more often than not, thank you for always having my back. I love you."

Those words had made the waterworks tap open and tears gush, so that when Ginny came over to and hugged them, they all sniffled in their group hug, trying hard not to break out into loud racking sobs.

As Ginny returned to her seat and they resumed eating, Ashleigh let her sister's words sink in. Even though she sometimes considered Ginny to be spoiled—this was more her fault than Ginny's—it was clear that Ginny was thoughtful and appreciative. She sincerely hoped that Ben Duckworth would be a worthy husband and make her sister the happiest woman when he married her.

After dinner, she and Eloise returned home, leaving Ginny and her friends to enjoy their stay at the hotel.

With a week to go to the wedding, the sisters had much to do.

The wedding would be small, with just friends and family. They had family coming from out of state and Ashleigh had made reservations for them to stay at the local bed and breakfast.

It was a given that Ginny wouldn't be working at all this week, so between the two of them, they had plenty to do, with taking care of guests who would be arriving a few days before Ginny's big day and making sure that things would be ticking over at the shop.

They asked all of their part-time assistants to come in as neither of them would be working on the day of the wedding.

Ashleigh had finished her usual Sunday morning yoga and was sitting in the backyard sipping a cold glass of water, when she heard the commotion. Someone was shouting. She turned and looked, before her heart almost exploded as she realized that it was Ginny. The color drained from her face as she jumped out of her seat and rushed to the door to find Eloise with her arms wrapped around a sobbing Ginny.

For the love of all things crazy, what on earth had happened now? Ginny was sobbing and babbling incoherently. They couldn't figure out what she was saying because her face was buried in Eloise's neck. Eloise looked at her, a criss-cross of angry lines on her face.

Ashleigh smoothed her hand over Ginny's hair, "Ginny, stop it now. Calm down. What's wrong?" Her first thought was that there had been a terrible accident at the hotel and that one of her friends had hurt themselves. This was always her first thought, ever since her parents' accident.

"It's off. It's off. I don't want to marry him."

Eloise raised an eyebrow, and Ashleigh's heart thundered. This wasn't about the girls or the hotel.

"What happened?" Her insides twisted into knots. She dreaded the answer.

"It's off." Ginny lifted her head, her eyes bloodshot, her nose snotty, her face bloated and red. Just then, a car screeched and ground to a halt outside.

"Don't let him in" she cried. "I don't want to see him again."

"Ben?" Eloise asked.

Ginny's body shook as she sobbed. "Don't let him in." Ashleigh looked through the curtains. It wasn't Ben. It was one of Ginny's close friends, Talia. She opened the door. A cab had pulled up outside and Talia climbed out. Ashleigh walked out, pulling the door partially closed so that Ginny wouldn't see. "What's happened?"

Talia's lips twitched. "Someone posted photos of Ben online, and one of the girls saw it and showed—"

"Ben? What photos?" Ashleigh demanded, her insides braced because she didn't want to hear this, but knew she had to.

"He was lying in bed with a topless woman."

"Oh, for goodness' sake!" Ashleigh cried out loud. The door opened and Eloise's eyes widened to saucer size. Ginny looked out.

"Let's go inside." Ashleigh pulled Talia into the house, not wanting to cause a scene that the neighbors might enjoy.

"He cheated on me," Ginny cried. "That's what he did." She wiped her nose with the back of her hand. "I told him not to go to that place but he said he wanted one crazy night."

"What?" Eloise snapped.

Ashleigh could hear the blood pounding in her ears. "What place?"

"Cooper's. It's a bar with … women … who collect tips, the size of which depend on how little they wear and how much they flirt," Talia began to explain.

"A strip club?" Eloise asked.

"Not quite. Not that bad. Just women in skimpy clothes."

Talia put her hand on Ginny's arm. "He might not have done anything. He might have been framed."

"I don't care," Ginny cried. "I don't care."

Eloise pulled out a few tissues from the box and handed to them to Ginny who blew her nose loudly. Eloise handed her another couple.

"How real does it look? The photo?" Eloise asked.

When Talia looked at the floor, they had their answer. She shrugged. "Who knows? It might have been a prank."

"Why are you taking his side?" Ginny asked.

Talia shrugged. "I'm just saying, don't go rushing to any hasty decisions."

"I know what I've seen. I don't care if he didn't sleep with her, he shouldn't have been in bed with her in the first place, not for one second. He didn't have to be there."

Ginny was right. It didn't matter if he'd slept with her or not … how would anyone ever know the truth? And knowing what she did about Ben, having met him and seen him first-hand, Ashleigh wasn't sure she could trust that man as far as she could throw him.

She pulled Talia into the hallway and motioned for Eloise to take Ginny into the kitchen. She asked Talia to run through what had happened once she and Eloise had left. It transpired that they had all been enjoying a lovely time in the Jacuzzi this morning, and then one of the girls from the group had shrieked out loudly. She'd been sitting on the bench, looking at her cell phone. Everyone got out of the Jacuzzi and swarmed around her. By the time they'd realized what was in the photos, they'd tried to keep it away from Ginny, but she had come over and demanded to see what they were looking at.

"It's not that we didn't want her to see it, we just didn't want her to get upset without us getting to the bottom of the truth first. Something like that can be shocking and a few of us wanted to find out what had happened from one of the guys there," Talia explained.

Ashleigh also wanted to get to the truth. Fast. "What do you think happened?" she asked Talia. But the girl stared at the floor, and it was a moment or two before her eyes looked up again, and directly at Ashleigh.

"One of the guys there, Rob, says that Ben had had too much to drink, and he was getting handsy with one of the waitresses."

Ashleigh's hand flew to her mouth.

"Rob said he tried to tell Ben to slow down, and to quit messing around, but Ben didn't take any notice, and the two men had an altercation. Rob isn't Ben's friend, he's Ginny's friend, but he and a few of us have been out with Ginny and Ben. Rob said he backed off because he saw that Ben was getting angry but also that Ben's friends were egging him on."

Ashleigh wiped her forehead with the back of her hand. What a mess. What a situation. What a thing to happen to her baby sister. She was livid inside, seething with a rage so red hot that her insides were in danger of spontaneously combusting.

"Does Rob think something happened?" She needed to know, but even what she had heard so far had raised enough alarm bells. The warning signs had gone off in her head long before today.

"He's not sure," whispered Talia. "Ginny became hysterical and we tried to calm her down, then she called Ben to tell him what she'd seen but he didn't answer his phone. I bet he was too scared to. She took a picture of the photo—it was on a social media site—and she sent that to him. As soon as he got that, he called her, and she told him it was off."

"He knows that she knows." Ashleigh's mind churned over the myriad of outcomes that could follow on from this.

"He knows. She turned her phone off, but she was crying uncontrollably. We couldn't stop her. She said she needed to go to her room and calm down, but the next thing we know is that she's gotten dressed and rushed out. I followed her as fast as I could."

"You did the right thing, Talia. Thank you."

"There's no need to thank me. I just hope Ginny is going to be okay. I feel so bad for her."

CHAPTER 20

*G*inny lay curled up on the sofa with a pillow. Eloise and Ashleigh fussed over her and had ordered her to turn her cell phone off. Ashleigh kept an eye on the door, in case any more of Ginny's friends showed up to check in on her. She'd told Talia to tell everyone not to call Ginny or come over as she obviously needed time to process things.

Inside, Ashleigh was heartbroken for her sister. She didn't know what to do or say that could make Ginny feel better. Could anything make her feel better, given the circumstances?

Ginny was adamant that the wedding was off, and secretly, Ashleigh and Eloise weren't too upset about this. It meant that they had a lot of phone calls to make; explaining to the wedding guests, as well as canceling many things, but this was preferable to Ginny walking down the aisle with a man they considered not worthy of her. In the long-term, this would be the better decision, but they were fearful knowing how quickly Ginny could be swayed, and how good Ben was at convincing her that he hadn't done anything wrong. What if Ben showed up and then tried to sweet talk her in order to explain the events away?

Ashleigh didn't doubt that he would blame the photos on a setup orchestrated by his friends.

Even if he hadn't slept with the woman, his behavior was unforgiveable. It would always be his word, and Ashleigh didn't trust him. She hoped Ginny wouldn't be won over as easily as last time.

"We were having such a nice time," Ginny murmured, finally saying something. They had been sitting in silence and Talia had left a short while ago. They had waited by her side, not wanting to pressure her and giving her some time to process events.

"Everything was going so well …" She blew her nose again. Ashleigh couldn't help but agree. It had been a lovely weekend, what with the spa treatments, the use of the Jacuzzi and the steam room and the pool, and dinner at The Connington. She hadn't had time off and indulged herself like that for the longest time. It had been exactly what she had needed, but now, that had all been forgotten. Now, it was painful to watch Ginny, broken and listless, lying on the sofa as if her world had ended. And in a way, it had.

"It had been such a great weekend, and the day before, having you two with me. We've never spent time having fun like that, together." She sniffled into her tissue.

Ashleigh stared at the patterned material of her yoga pants. They didn't spend time together, the three of them, doing fun things. They were always at work together, and when it came to leisure time, they all did their own thing. Ginny's bachelorette weekend had been an opportunity for them to unwind, relax and indulge themselves.

Ashleigh had slept like a baby.

But now that this had happened, the memories of that time-- that one day--would be forever tainted.

She started to cry again, this time silently. Big, fat tears rolled down her cheeks.

"Stop that now," said Eloise, kneeling on the floor and patting her arm. "We'll have other fun times." She glanced over her shoulder at Ashleigh. "We'll make time to do fun things."

"I don't know what to do about the house," said Ginny, hugging a pillow closer to her. She sniffled noisily. "We spent so much time picking everything for the rooms, deciding on the colors."

Ashleigh was itching to remind her that he had upset her over a lamp, but she'd managed to keep her mouth closed.

"He can be really nice sometimes, but … but ..." And the tears started again.

Ashleigh walked over and sat on the sofa, near Ginny's feet. Words couldn't comfort her. Only time could. "We're here for you, Ginny." She struggled to find the right words to put her sister's mind at ease, but she couldn't, because there were no words. What he'd done had been unforgiveable.

"We had so much fun after breakfast. No one wanted to go home and we wished we had another night. Then Talia suggested we go sit in the Jacuzzi. And then ..." Ginny's lower lip started to tremble again. "I saw a few of my friends huddled around Talia. She wasn't in the Jacuzzi, but sitting on the side, looking at her phone. Then I heard them gasping, but then one of them said something like 'she can't see this,' I think, but when they all looked at me, I knew." Ginny rubbed her sore eyes which were red from all the crying. "I got out and went right over to them and demanded to see whatever it was they were looking at. Then someone said I shouldn't see it, and Talia said I had a right to know, and she showed me. It was ... Ben... lying next to a … a… a woman." She sniffled again, struggling to regain her composure. Ashleigh squeezed her arm gently in a show of support. "They were both topless and fast asleep, and then there was a video recording. Ben wakes up, he swears and the woman wakes up and there's pandemonium."

"There was a recording?" Eloise cried.

"And photos, but I saw the recording. There was no denying what had gone on."

"Oh, Ginny." Both sisters leaned over and hugged Ginny, as awkward as it was with her lying down.

The Rose sisters were doomed, wedding-wise, marriage-wise, romance-wise.

Ginny felt like an idiot. Like someone who should have known better. And she should have. She'd had plenty of clues as to what Ben was like. But she had brushed them off, because he made her laugh, and he was so good-looking, and so nice to her. At least, he had been in the beginning, but what with everything to do with the wedding, and the pressures of his work, he'd seemed stressed and she'd started to see a different side to him.

Her uneasiness with Ben hadn't happened in a heartbeat, it had crept up on her slowly. He was a lovely guy, he had been, he *was*. But the sum of all the little bits of nastiness he had shown in recent months, when considered together, were too hard to ignore.

And now this had happened. She had been humiliated in front of her friends with the proof being seen by everyone. It wasn't just photos and a video recording of a couple in bed, it was of a man on his bachelor party; a man who was getting married *next week*.

It was a story, perfect for the picking for all the gossipmongers out there.

Her sisters, the true backbone of her life, weren't judging or lecturing her or telling her what she should do. They were exactly what she'd said last night when she had made a toast to them— they were the best sisters she could have ever hoped for, and now she was going to have to let them down.

There had been so much planning put into the wedding, and

the dress. Oh, the beautiful, gorgeous, silk and delicate lace dress, not to mention the cake, and the honeymoon and the flowers.

And the house. Their new home. The one they had painted and decorated together. The home they were supposed to start their new life in. What would they do about that?

"I'm going to bed," she said, even thought it was only the afternoon. Such a terrible messy ending to what should have been a prelude leading up to one of the most important and cherished days of her life.

Maybe this was a blessing in disguise, to find out now. Imagine saying her vows, marrying Ben, and finding out on her honeymoon, or afterwards? She needed time to herself, she needed her sisters to have some peace and quiet to themselves. She got up. "I need to think and make a final decision. I know we don't have much time."

"Take all the time you need, honey," said Eloise.

"You decide what you want to do, Ginny. We'll stand by you, but remember, you deserve the best. You have to ask yourself if Ben is the best for you?"

She pressed her lips together. Ashleigh had made a point she couldn't stop thinking about, and as she climbed the stairs wearily, her bones and heart heavy, she already knew the answer to that question.

CHAPTER 21

"*I* want to talk to her," he shouted, craning his neck over Ashleigh's shoulder.

"She doesn't want to talk to you." Ashleigh positioned herself directly in front of him, holding the door only half open to make it very clear that he wasn't welcome here.

"Ginny!" he shouted, ignoring them.

"Didn't you hear?" Eloise growled. "She doesn't want to talk to you."

"I want to talk to her."

"She doesn't want to talk to you," they both cried at the same time. He looked shocked, and took a step back before pointing his finger at them, his face twisting. "You've never liked me. The pair of you, you've always had it out for me. You think she's too good for me." He jabbed his index finger at them.

Ashleigh kept her cool. Whoever this rude little upstart was, she was going to keep her sister safe and out of this man's way. Maybe things turning out like this had been a blessing in disguise, and she hoped that Ginny would make the right decision.

"It doesn't matter what we think of you, what you need to

remember is that Ginny doesn't want to see you," she said, her tone even as she glared daggers at him.

"I love her and we're getting married!"

"I wouldn't be so sure about that." She was seething with rage inside, and it was a miracle that she had managed to stay so calm when what she really wanted to do was to slam the door in his face.

She hoped Ginny wouldn't give in to him. No doubt she could hear the commotion from her bedroom. What Ben had done was deplorable, and Ginny had every right to dump him.

Privately, Ashleigh hoped her sister would make the wise choice—the only right choice—and do what was best for her. A life with this brute standing in front of her didn't seem like the option that would give her that.

"Ginny! Ginny! Get down here. I wanna talk to you!" he hollered at the top of his lungs.

"Shut the hell up and get lost." Ashleigh snapped, her poise and calm cracking.

"And if I don't, what are you gonna do about it?"

"I will do what I need to. You watch me."

"Go on. Get lost!" Eloise threatened.

Ashleigh's nostrils flared, her mouth twisting and pinching as she tried to find the right words to hurl at him. "If you don't get your abusive little carcass away from here, I'll call the police."

"You wouldn't."

"Try me." Her words were only putting more fuel on the fire. In the back of her mind was the distinct possibility that Ginny might relent and soften, and give in to him. What if she went ahead with the wedding? Where would that leave her and Eloise, who had now laid bare their hatred of Ben?

"Just go." Eloise sounded weary.

"I'm not giving up on her," he warned. "I love Ginny, and she loves me."

Not anymore. The words were on the tip of Ashleigh's tongue, but she held back, exercising the utmost restraint. She breathed a sigh of relief when he got into his car and drove away.

They closed the door, and turned all the locked, before collapsing into a heap on the sofas.

It was still early afternoon, but it felt as if the day had stretched out to evening.

"What are we going to do?" Eloise asked again, and once again, Ashleigh had no answer.

"Ginny said she'll give us a decision in the morning," she replied finally. "Let's at least give her that time." Though time was the one thing they were running out of.

The sound of Ben's voice made Ginny flinch.

He was outside, and he was calling for her. For an insane minute, she felt a pull on her heart and she considered giving in and putting a Band-Aid over the whole thing. It wasn't so much that she loved him; she was still livid with rage, but she had seen a nicer, kinder side to him.

Once.

She was sure that better side was still there, somewhere. She also didn't want to let people down. The wedding, the guests, all the work that had gone into the wedding preparations. All that time, money and effort.

But she recoiled at the thought of being near him, and as she recalled the photo of him with the other woman, she could taste bile in her throat. It was when he got into his car and drove away that she let out the breath she didn't realize she'd been holding.

She curled up in the fetal position on the bed again, hugging herself and wishing that this sleazy episode hadn't happened. But it had. She could never unsee what she had seen. Could never forget it, nor the fact that her friends and sisters had seen it, too.

Her entire world had been upended in one moment.

CHAPTER 22

The next day, they waited on pins and needles while having breakfast.

"Should we wake her?" Eloise asked.

"No, let her sleep. Who knows how much sleep she managed to get?" Ashleigh had checked in on her before she she'd gone to bed later that night. "We should get to work. She'll let us know when she's ready to face things." Ashleigh cleared the table and loaded the dishwasher.

"I'll drive," Eloise offered, releasing a heavy sigh. Ashleigh felt the weariness. She hadn't slept much at all, and had lain in bed, tossing and thinking. While her heart ached for Ginny and her predicament, she was also aware that her idea of telling Eloise had been thwarted.

It meant more delay. Which was fine. She wouldn't do anything, she wasn't about to leave Ginny now, not while she was dealing with this. But all the same, it felt as if this waiting and delaying, and wishing and dreaming had been the blueprint for her entire life.

As she went to open the door, Ginny came racing down the stairs. "You were going to leave without me?"

Ashleigh spun around to find Ginny all dressed and ready to leave. Her heart sank. Her sister was back to normal. Looking strong and as if nothing had happened. She had obviously heard him yelling for her yesterday, and Ashleigh didn't put it past that little weasel to have called Ginny and convinced her that he'd been framed or something. He'd likely fed Ginny a line, and she'd stupidly fallen for it.

"Where do you think you're going?" she asked, dreading the answer.

"To work."

"What? Why?" Eloise asked. "You don't have to. You can take it easy for a few days."

Ginny stood in the hallway. "I've made my decision, and it's off. I'm not marrying Ben."

Ashleigh's heart jumped and a warmth radiated through her at this. "Are you sure, Ginny?"

"Do you need more time?" Eloise asked.

"We don't have a lot of time," Ashleigh reminded them.

Eloise gave her a narrowed-eye stare. "We can delay the wedding."

Delay it for what? Ashleigh didn't like the way Eloise was handling this. "After what happened, Ginny knows what she wants to do. I don't think any amount of time is going to make a difference."

"I couldn't sleep all night. I maybe got a couple of hours sleep, but I woke up and I knew I didn't want to go through with it. Not with Ben. I can't marry him. Even if I hadn't seen that picture, and he hasn't done anything—I don't think he did anything, but I'll never know. That's the problem. I'll always have that doubt, and I don't want to get married with any seed of a doubt in my head. I wasn't happy when he told me he was going to Cooper's. I told him I didn't like the idea of it, but he didn't care what I thought. He wanted a crazy night, and that's what he got."

Ashleigh glanced at her watch then leaned against the closed door. "Do you want to sit here a while and talk about it? We've got time."

"No. It's business as usual. I don't want to mope around feeling sorry for myself because that won't fix anything, or mend my heart."

"Do you still love him?" Ashleigh asked.

"Yes, I can't fall out of love with him, just like that. I still love him, but I'm angry and I hate him, too. I know he's not good for me, and it's not only this thing. Ben's upset me on a few occasions, on a lot of occasions, actually."

"Oh, Ginny." A little piece of Ashleigh's heart broke. "Why didn't you say anything? I guessed something wasn't quite right lately, I mean. Sometimes I could tell from just looking at your face that things weren't going smoothly, and then you came home crying a few weeks ago and I knew it wasn't my imagination."

"How long have you been having doubts, Gin?"

Ginny's gaze dropped to the floor. "Maybe once we were engaged. I think he felt the pressure. Something changed between us. He would do or say things that weren't nice, but I kept disregarding them each time he upset me. He wasn't the kind and thoughtful man I had fallen in love with. He'd changed. I don't know if it's the pressure of the wedding, or his work…"

"Don't make excuses for him," Ashleigh said gently. Women were so prone to making excuses for their men, and she was pretty sure men wouldn't make the same excuses if the roles were reversed. How jaded she had become.

Ginny looked at them both in turn. "I'm sorry I put you both through this."

"Put us through what?" Eloise asked.

"You haven't put us through anything, Ginny. Don't be silly."

Ashleigh put her arms around her sister and held her tight, thankful that she had made the right decision.

"But now we have so much to clear up, and cancel, and tell everyone. We won't get deposits back for a lot of things."

"We'll take care of it," Eloise reassured her.

"Don't you worry about a thing. We'll take care of it." The money didn't matter, what mattered was that Ginny had made her own decision, and she was holding up fine. She was stronger than Ashleigh had expected.

"But the wedding, and the reception, the honeymoon, and ... uh... the dress." Her face crumpled. "My beautiful dress." Ginny raked a hand through her hair. "And the house," she said softly. "We spent so long choosing everything, and painting and decorating it."

"There'll be other houses," Ashleigh said.

"And there'll be other men," quipped Eloise with a grin, until Ashleigh narrowed her eyes at her.

"I'm going to work today, maybe in a few hours' time. I need to get myself together, and speak to my friends. I left them at the hotel and they've been calling and texting. I need to let them know."

"You don't even have to come in," Ashleigh said, not understanding Ginny's unshakeable determination to want to be at work at a time like this.

"It will distract me. I'll take care of things in the shop, if you two can take care of the cancelations and tell everyone."

They hugged again, another group hug, like the one they'd had after Ginny had made that wonderful speech, but this time it was for a completely different reason.

CHAPTER 23

*a*nd so it began, the Herculean task of canceling all the wedding preparations and the hotel reservations for their family. Telling everyone without explaining the real reason in detail was heavy and hard, and Ashleigh and Eloise approached it like a marathon, something that was painful but which had to be gone through and completed.

It was the dent to Ginny's heart, the damage Ben had done to her, that Ashleigh was worried about. The way it had happened, the public humiliation, would wound anyone, but Ginny especially. She was sensitive, as well as being occasionally spoiled and a little too wrapped up in herself at times. What Ben had done was what no woman should ever have to experience and suffer through.

They would have to keep an eye on her.

"I'm worried about her," Eloise said, having canceled the hotel reservations.

Ashleigh pinched the bridge of her nose. She had just come off the phone from telling some of the guests. "We'll have to keep a tighter eye on her, that's all."

"Maybe I'll cut down my vacation."

"What vacation?" Ashleigh wasn't sure she'd heard right.

"Beth's wedding. In Hyannis Port. I said I'd take a week off for it."

So she had. It had slipped right out of her mind. Beth's wedding was taking place the week following what would have been Ginny's wedding.

"A week?" Ashleigh echoed. "After the wedding day? Aren't the newlyweds going on their honeymoon?"

"Not right away."

Ashleigh let out a heavy breath. Eloise had recently come back from Las Vegas, and then she'd enjoyed the night at The Connington, and now she was off again, enjoying another week of vacation in Hyannis Port. The woman was having everyone's share of fun all to herself.

Ashleigh longed for escape, too, but the way things were going, she wasn't even going to get a chance to tell her sisters that she needed to take a few months off. Her hopes of telling Eloise had been dashed, and now it was out of the question. She didn't want to upset the status quo, knowing that Ginny was fragile and had experienced such a humiliating breakup, and with the wedding being called off, it wouldn't be the right time to make her announcement of wanting to leave and travel to Europe.

Once again, her dreams would have to take a backseat.

"I'll come back after the wedding then, if it makes you feel better." Eloise offered. It was tempting to tell her to. But why should she? Surely Eloise could see that Ginny would be upset, and maybe, as a sister, she could come back after a few days and be here for her, instead of leaving Ashleigh to take care of things as usual.

"It's up to you," she replied.

"Okay, well, yeah, sure. I might consider it."

Consider it?

Ashleigh wanted to put her out of her misery. "Stick to your plans. There's no point in you getting all sad and moody, just because Ginny is."

"Who said I'm sad and moody?" The sound of Ginny's voice made them feel guilty. They hadn't heard Ginny come into the office. It was almost lunchtime but Ashleigh had hoped she'd at least take the day off today. Nursing a bruised heart and having to face people wasn't an easy task.

"I meant that you're not exactly going to be all happy and smiling," Ashleigh said hurriedly.

Ginny walked over to her desk and turned on her computer. "I'm okay. I'm going to be fine."

"Eloise is going to Hyannis Port ..." Ashleigh started to explain.

"Do you want to come?" Eloise asked, giving Ashleigh a sideways glance. She seemed to think this was a brilliant idea. "I'm sure Beth wouldn't mind. You can be my plus one, since I don't have one."

"And go to a wedding?" Ashleigh asked, her voice tight. Sometimes Eloise didn't think. At all.

As if it had hit her like a ten-ton truck, Eloise's eyes grew wide. "Oh, right. No, no, you wouldn't want to come and see—"

"See someone getting married? No, I wouldn't," Ginny told her.

Ashleigh turned on her sister. "Do you ever think about the words *before* they leave your mouth?"

"I was trying to be helpful," Eloise protested.

"Try a little harder."

"Okay, I'm sorry. I was trying to help."

"His parents keep calling me." Ginny said it so quietly that at first it didn't register.

Ashleigh's heart sank. "What?"

"They want to know what's going on. He's obviously told them."

"I bet he hasn't told them why the wedding's off," Eloise snarled.

"I'll call them." This wasn't for Ginny to deal with, talking to his parents and explaining the situation. They had a right to know, but it wasn't for Ginny to explain. As the oldest sister, Ashleigh would take care of it. "I'll speak to them. Don't you worry about a thing."

"Thanks." Ginny looked as if she was about to cry, and hurriedly left the room. Eloise started to go after her.

"Leave her," Ashleigh cautioned. "She needs time and she probably doesn't need you and me every second to comfort her."

Eloise's hand went to her hips. "I'll give her twenty minutes."

"We have to find something to do with her this weekend," said Ashleigh, rubbing her brow. "She's going to have the wedding on her mind and we need to distract her."

"Let's take the day off. We were going to anyway. Let's do something fun!"

That was a great idea. "Yes, we were going to take the day off." They'd arranged for their assistants to take care of things in their absence. "I think we need to go away. She won't want to hang around Whisper Falls and be reminded of everything."

"Starling Bay," cried Eloise, clicking her fingers.

"Perfect." Ashleigh had fond memories of the small coastal town. They had visited with their parents a few times, and she and Ford had visited it back when they had been dating. "I'm going out for lunch later," she announced. She'd called Darcie earlier and arranged to meet. She wanted to tell her what had happened, before Darcie heard it from the townspeople and the usual rumor mill.

But, more than that, she wanted to talk it over with her best friend, because she had no one else to share her troubles with.

CHAPTER 24

"*C*an we talk?"

Ginny spun around to find Ben staring at her. He had snuck up on her. She glanced around the shop for signs of Ashleigh or Eloise, but couldn't see them. Her pulse started to race. "You shouldn't be here. Ashleigh will throw you out."

"In front of the customers?" he snorted. "Doubt it."

She knew she had to face him, and she was going to in the next few days, she was working up to it. She hadn't expected him to come here of all places. Her heart felt as if it was stumbling all over the place inside her chest. Her breathing turned fast and shallow.

"What do you want?"

"I'm sorry. I want to make it up to you. I just want you to know that nothing happened with that woman. I would never do that to you, Ginny." He tried to take hold of her hands, but she stepped back, the thought of his touching her disgusted her. Things could never be the same between them now. Ever. He had broken the trust.

"A picture doesn't lie. And whether you 'did' anything or not,

I'll never know. Even if you 'did' nothing," she air quoted the 'did', "what I saw was bad enough. Even if that naked woman—"

"She wasn't naked. She was wearing shorts."

"What?" Ginny couldn't believe his response, or that he was defending her attire. "Even if she been reading you a bedtime story, naked, *like that*," she continued, wrinkling her face in disgust, "what you did was completely unacceptable."

"I was an idiot." He punched the display table.

"Stop that!"

A customer stared at them. She remembered that Ashleigh had gone to lunch. Where was Eloise?

"I didn't sleep with her."

"You were so drunk, how would you even remember what you did?"

His eyes narrowed with suspicion. "Who told you I was drunk?"

"Does it matter?" she cried. "You told me you wanted one crazy night."

"That's not what I meant by it. I wanted to have one night of drinking and playing pool and hanging around with my friends."

"As if I was going to stop you from any of that after we got married."

"I miss you, Ginny. I messed things up, I know I did, but I swear to you nothing happened. The guys were just having some fun."

"The guys? You're blaming them for this?"

"They were goofing around. They told her to get into bed with me. I was drunk, out like a light. They planted her there."

She scoffed, her disbelief shooting through the roof. "Your friends 'planted' this woman in your bed?"

"Yeah," he nodded vigorously. "And then they took a picture. How stupid do you think I'd have to be to let something like that happen?"

"About as stupid as you were to want to go to Cooper's and have your one night of crazy. I'd say you definitely got exactly what you wanted. A night of crazy. Was it worth it?"

He seemed knocked back, his shoulders slumping, and his face downcast. "I'll make it up to you, Ginny. I swear I will. Nothing did happen. I promise you. Let me make it up to you."

"You can never make it up to me."

"Can you please leave?" Ashleigh appeared out of thin air, her face dark. Her sister stared at her in concern.

"Just give us a few moments, please, Ashleigh," Ginny pleaded. Ashleigh gave Ben a menacing look.

"I'm watching you," she hissed. "Keep your voices down," she said to Ginny.

"She never liked me." Ben grumbled, running his fingers down the sleeve of a wedding dress on a mannequin.

"Keep your hands off," Ginny snapped. He was like an errant child, not the twenty-six-year-old he was supposed to be, blaming everyone and anyone for his woes.

"What do you want, Ben? Why are you here? If it's about the house, Ashleigh is going to speak to your parents about it." They would have to sell it, recoup what each party had put into it and split the profits, if there were any.

"I don't care about the house. I love you, Ginny. We made that house into a home. Don't do this."

"I didn't do anything. *You* did. You need to cancel the catering and the hotel for the reception. Eloise says she tried to, but the booking was made in your name." It surprised her how calm she felt, saying this to him, instead of breaking into pieces in front of his eyes.

"This is it? You're really calling off the wedding?"

"There's no coming back from this, Ben. How can you not see that?"

125

"Don't do this, Ginny. I'm the biggest idiot going, and I don't know what came over me—"

"You *do* know what came over you. It was a naked woman. That's what came over you."

He blinked at her retort, his face meshing into a confused expression. She wasn't going to stand here and let him pretend he'd been blameless in this. There was no bigger and more glaring evidence of what Ben had done, and how he had messed up, than what she and her friends had seen. He would never be able to excuse his behavior.

It wasn't just what had happened on that night. Now that she'd experienced the lightning strike of that event which had scarred her, it had also opened her eyes to everything else she had suppressed and explained away in the past. His controlling behavior, the way he spoke to her sometimes, his personality and emotionally abusive ways; there seemed to be a growing list of things about him that bothered her and these had become more prevalent as the wedding day drew near. There was no point opening this big can of worms by telling him because he would only make up more lies and excuses and she was done with listening.

"You're splitting up with me?" His voice was so low, it was almost a whisper. But the way he said it, with those sad puppy-dog eyes, it hit the arrow right in her Achilles' heel. She was in danger of giving in and letting him apologize and make up. But the photo of him in bed with the woman flashed into her mind again, hitting her like a second lightning strike.

She would never be able to wipe that image away. She'd never be able to trust him. The onus to make up and prove that he was going to change was on him, not her, and for now, the wedding, like their relationship, was off.

"Yes."

"But I love you."

"If you loved me, you wouldn't have done what you did."

His face twisted, and he looked at her as if he didn't understand. And that was the problem.

He didn't.

His lips turned up at the corners like a snarl and he stomped off, slamming the door so hard, the reverberations lingered.

She'd done the right thing, but why did she feel so sad all of a sudden? Up until this moment, she had been stronger than she'd thought she would be. Her reaction had even surprised her, but maybe it was because she had started to recall the things that had happened between them; all the recent arguments and disagreements. It had dawned on her that deep down, she had secretly wondered what she was letting herself in for but had been too afraid to confront it head on.

Ben had done her a favor and made things easier. She wasn't a delicate doll made of fine bone china, she was much stronger than she had realized. She had rushed in too quickly when this good-looking, muscular guy had bumped into her at the cinema, causing her popcorn to tip all over the floor. One look into his smoldering green eyes and she'd fallen for him. When he'd apologized, and brought her another, bigger bag of popcorn, and then walked away, she couldn't help but keep looking over at him.

They got talking, and she became smitten.

The Ben she had met then was a long way away from the man he was now. Seventeen months, from meeting to getting married. What had she been thinking?

Her sisters looked over at her, and she nodded, indicating that she was fine. But she wasn't. An unexpected feeling of sadness seeped through her pores, and she longed to be alone, with her thoughts and her misery. She disappeared into the storeroom at the back. But the first thing she saw, hanging up on the wall was her wedding dress. Her heart ricocheted inside her chest as memories of happiness sliced through the deceit, creating a fast and furious collage of her life with Ben.

She had envisioned herself slipping into this dress and walking down the aisle with Ben after they had been married. She had imagined walking with him and seeing all their friends and family. He had truly made her feel special, and at the start he had made her laugh, and they had shared a lot of the same ideals and dreams. But somewhere along the way, she had seen the kinks in their relationship, so tiny at first, she barely noticed. He would say or do something that made her stop. A nasty comment about a fellow coworker, rage about his boss. She had assumed he was feeling frustrated about his job. He hated what he did and she had tried to help him look elsewhere, but he didn't seem to want to do anything to fix the problem, preferring to rail against things instead.

But in recent months, his anger had flared a little too often, and was often directed at her. And for things that were minor. It was the house, buying their new house together that had started it all. She had assumed that he was worried about the financing, but their families had helped them out, and they weren't going to be making payments they couldn't afford.

It wasn't the money, it was that he liked to control every little thing, from the color of the walls to the new appliances.

Her dreams of building a cosy little home together started to crumble as she began to see another side to him. And then he started to question out loud whether they were rushing into marriage.

He would make off-the-cuff remarks about his days as a free man coming to a close, lamenting that at the age of twenty-six, he was too young to settle down.

That had been the hardest to hear, but it had come off the back of an argument they'd had about buying a new refrigerator.

Silly things. This wasn't the Ben she had fallen in love with.

She ran her thumb over the tiny little buttons on the back of the dress. Eloise and Ashleigh had told her that these would be a nightmare to do up, but she'd had her own way, opting for a long row of buttons from her back all the way down. And they did look beautiful. The lace looked pretty too. She tried not to dwell on the fact that Ben would not have liked that she would have had a bare back, exposing too much of her skin.

"It's a pretty dress," said Eloise, coming up and putting her arm around her shoulder.

"It was." But now she felt that everything about it was full of sad, bad memories for her.

"It still is. What do you want to do with it?" Ashleigh asked, slipping her arm around Ginny's waist.

"Sell it. Someone will buy it." It was of no use to her.

"Are you sure?" Ashleigh asked.

"I don't want us to lose any more money on it, and I'm never going to wear it."

Her sisters hugged her, making her feel loved and special in a way that only sisters could. "Don't worry about losing money. We won't," Ashleigh told her. "There will be another dress for you, when the time is right."

"When the man is right," Eloise piped in, as tactless as ever.

CHAPTER 25

*A*shleigh made sure Ginny was on the shop floor all of the time, in an effort to keep her away from the office and the store room. She and Eloise had packed away Ginny's wedding dress and hadn't yet decided what to do with it. They both agreed that it needed to be out of Ginny's sight.

Since Ginny refused to go home, they had one eye on their work and the customers and the other eye on their sister. But to all accounts and purposes, Ginny seemed to be handling events well. In the evenings, she'd been meeting with her friends who all fussed around her and tried to distract her.

Ashleigh had completed the arduous task of meeting with Ben's parents briefly, and had let them know of the events that had transpired from Ginny's point of view. They were shocked, and devastated, because they loved Ginny. They seemed hopeful that one day, in the not too distant future, Ben and Ginny might reconcile.

'Over my dead body' had been Ashleigh's first thought.

On Saturday morning, on what would have been Ginny's wedding day, they drove to Starling Bay, a small town an hour or so away, hoping to keep Ginny occupied and not dwelling on what would have been. As soon as they arrived there, they went to a diner and had a lovely brunch.

Eloise was adamant that this was the place where a celebrity chef had staged a TV show last year, but Ashleigh didn't know what she was talking about. Neither did Ginny.

Later they went for a long stroll by the beach, talking about anything, vacations, possible trips that they could make, doing more things together, instead of always being stuck at the shop.

"Like last week," said Eloise. "At The Connington, having those beauty treatments and then having the pool and Jacuzzi—" She stopped talking eventually, even though Ashleigh had been trying to catch her eye ever since she opened her mouth and said, 'Last week.'

It seemed as if no subject was safe.

"I'd like to go somewhere far," said Ashleigh, hoping to move the conversation to somewhere far from Ginny's wedding woes.

"Like where?" Ginny asked.

"Oh, I don't know," Ashleigh replied, even though she did. Her itinerary was coming together nicely.

"You, go traveling?" Eloise asked, as if Ashleigh had said she wanted to fly to Mars.

"Yes, me, travel." Ashleigh tried to keep her tone neutral. "You're not the only one who can."

Eloise glared at her, appearing offended by the statement. "But you don't. You've never mentioned it. You've never gone anywhere."

"Because I've never ... I've never had the chance."

"Why not?"

"Because ... of the ... shop." Saying it out loud, it sounded feeble.

"But *we're* here."

"Yeah. We're here," Ginny replied.

She felt cornered. She knew they were here, but ... well, what could she say? That she didn't trust them? That she felt she was tied to the shop and didn't want to hand over the responsibility to them?

"There's nothing stopping you from going," Eloise persisted. She had an edge to her voice, as if she'd picked up on something that Ashleigh had intimated.

"Sixty-four flavors of ice cream." Ginny pointed to a shop over Ashleigh's shoulder.

"Can't be," murmured Eloise.

"We should go," suggested Ashleigh, grateful to have an end to the conversation. They walked over to the ice cream shop, which was something that she remembered from years ago. She had come here with their parents. The memory brought a lump to her throat.

"Ashleigh, what's wrong?" Ginny peered at her, her face a picture of worry.

"And don't say 'nothing.'" Eloise jabbed a finger in her direction.

"I was thinking of the times we'd come here with Mom and Dad."

They all fell silent, until Eloise asked, "This place has been here all that time?"

"I don't remember coming here."

Ashleigh ran her hand through Ginny's hair, ruffling it up. "You were too young to remember."

The silence blanketed them, cocooning them into their individual memories and thoughts.

"We didn't come here to be sad," said Ashleigh, determined not to have this day be gloomy. "I'm guessing they probably do multiple flavors of chocolate, right?"

"Ooooh." Eloise took the hint and joined in. "Sixty-four flavors, Gin. How many scoops are you going to have?"

Ginny gave a weak smile. "I don't know."

"Don't be like that." Ashleigh jabbed her gently in the arm. "You love ice cream!"

"And I can eat all I want now that I don't have to worry about fitting in a wedding dress."

Pin-drop silence ensued, until Ginny laughed. "It's okay to talk about it. I'm still here, we're still here. My heart might be a little bruised, but each time I think of those pictures of Ben with that woman …"

"Yuck." Eloise almost spat the word out.

"Clutched from the jaws of death." Ashleigh hooked her arm through Ginny's on one side, and Eloise did the same on the other, and the three of them marched up to the ice cream parlor.

They drove to Lake Ivanhoe later, and walked through the forest before going over to a gift store which stocked an amazing array of handmade and other gift items. Eloise couldn't stop stroking the owner's dog, a Great Dane named Spartacus. In the evening, they went to Fellini's, a lovely authentic Italian restaurant in town.

By the time they drove back, it was late, but they'd spent the day well, and had a treasure trove of new memories to cherish, completely overwriting what might have been.

CHAPTER 26

The trip to Starling Bay had done wonders for them all. They all woke up late the next day, and then made a huge breakfast together and ate it out in the backyard.

There was no wedding talk, or sadness from Ginny. She hid it well, thought Ashleigh, and she still continued to worry about her. Eloise was keeping an eye on Ginny too, but she also had her eye on her friend's upcoming wedding.

Back at the shop, it was business as usual. In this way they were lucky that they all worked together, because then they could keep a watchful eye on Ginny.

They received news from two happy customers. One of their brides had sent them a wonderful 'Thank you' card and the bride who had lost lots of weight, and for whom they'd had to open the shop on the Sunday, sent them a beautiful bouquet of flowers with a 'Thank you' note attached.

"This is what makes all of this so worthwhile," said Ashleigh, sighing as she pinned the 'Thank you cards' to a large board on one of the walls in the office. She arranged the flowers into a huge glass vase and put them near the service counter.

Eloise left for Hyannis Port early on Friday morning, leaving

Ginny and Ashleigh to take care of things in her absence. Ashleigh was determined to keep her sister busy and it was nice having just her and Ginny spend more time together. In the past, Ginny had often been out with Ben and this was the first time in a long time that she was at home in the evenings when they got back from work.

Spending all day at the shop, working together and then living together, it was surprising that they hadn't pulled one another's hair out. Darcie was often surprised that their arrangement worked as well as it seemed to.

They were sisters. It was a given that they would argue, and bicker and fall out. That's what sisters did. To not do that wouldn't make for a healthy sisterly relationship.

With just the two of them at home in the evening, they made dinner and ate together, before snuggling up on the sofa watching TV. Ashleigh kept waiting for Ginny to talk more about Ben, and about how she felt, but Ginny said nothing on that subject. Ginny had surprised them all. She was handling things better than expected, and she hadn't missed much time off work.

The saddest Ashleigh had seen her was when Ginny had been looking at her wedding dress. Apart from that, there had been the odd nights she'd heard her sister crying in bed. A couple of times Ashleigh had knocked on her door, but Ginny had called out to say that she was fine.

Ashleigh understood that this was something Ginny needed to get through in her own time. She had shared that she felt she'd done the right thing. She was glad that something had happened now instead of later on, after she and Ben had married, when it would have been harder to extricate herself from the relationship. It almost seemed like a blessing that Ben's true colors had been exposed.

In the evenings, they sat and talked, long after having finished their dinner.

"I'm tired." Ashleigh yawned, then stretched, before putting her hand over her glass when Ginny tried to refill it.

"It's Saturday night. Go on, do something daring. Let your hair down," Ginny urged her. Ashleigh relented and moved her hand.

Ginny refilled her glass. "Thanks for taking care of me."

Ashleigh lifted her glass to her lips and frowned. This had come out of nowhere. "I'll always take care of you, Ginny. Me and Eloise both."

"I know you do and you will, but you put everything aside and you've always been here. Always. I can't remember Eloise being here all the time."

"It's what sisters do," Ashleigh said softly.

"It's what moms and dads do." Something in Ginny's expression softened. And all of a sudden her eyes welled with tears.

"Ginny." Ashleigh set her glass down. "What is it? Why are you so upset?"

"I … I just… I don't know. I just feel so sad."

Ashleigh kissed the top of Ginny's head. "I was wondering when they would come, your tears. You need to let them out. It's okay to feel sad. There are better times ahead, just remember that."

Ginny placed her hand over Ashleigh's and sniffled. "I don't remember Mom and Dad, but I miss them. I look at their photos and I miss them and I can *feel* them. I've been feeling sad because of everything that's happened, and because I've realized that family is everything. And then I want to cry because I realize how much you've both done for me. Especially you, Ashleigh, you've done so much."

Ashleigh moved over to the chair next to Ginny. "I've done what any sister would have done."

"But you missed out on your life, and starting a family, because of me."

"I changed direction, but I wouldn't have had it any other way. You would have done the same if you'd been in my shoes."

"Do you regret it?"

She had regrets, but she didn't regret splitting up with Ford, letting him go, so that he could pursue his life. Just like she didn't regret being here for her sisters. "No. Never."

Ginny squeezed her hand. "I don't know what I would have done without you and Eloise."

"You won't ever have to because Eloise and I aren't ever leaving your side." They were silent, and then Ashleigh, trying to inject some lightness into the air, lifted Ginny's glass and handed it to her. Lifting her own glass up, she announced, "To better times ahead for all of us." They clinked glasses. She took a sip and sat back.

"Is that why you never go anywhere?" Ginny asked. "You're always here. I don't remember you going anywhere and leaving me and Eloise alone."

Ashleigh opened her mouth but didn't know what to say. Why had she stayed? Only taking a few days off here and there, for when Darcie had gotten married, and when she'd wanted to do nothing but sleep in and take it easy. Nothing had stopped her from leaving Whisper Falls, as Eloise had pointed out the other day.

"Well, you know." She shrugged. She had taken her allotted weeks of vacation off every year, but she hadn't gone anywhere, just puttered around the house or visited places nearby. And now that she had this big idea of leaving for a few months, she'd been unable to tell anyone but Darcie about it.

"Don't you ever wish you could take off, like Eloise?" Ginny asked.

"I've been thinking, about places I'd like to visit."

"This is this the first you've mentioned it. You've never said that before. What places?"

Ashleigh shrugged. "Europe."

"Europe? Where in Europe?"

"All of it. France, Italy, Spain. Greece, and England, too."

"Ashleigh!" Ginny laughed. "I never knew that was something you wanted to do! Listen to yourself. Why has this been such a big secret?"

"It's something I was going to do."

"With Ford, you mean?"

It was no secret that she and Ford had had plans, and that everything had changed for her on that fatal day. "We were going to travel for six months. That's a long time for me to go away now."

"Is that why you want to travel now? Because you feel like you missed out?" Ginny was hitting so close to the truth, it was scary.

Ashleigh took a big gulp of her wine. "I feel like I missed out on a lot of things."

"Like settling down, and getting married and stuff?" Ginny prompted. Ashleigh took another sip.

"I don't know about the settling down." She had these types of conversations with Eloise sometimes, but never with Ginny, who she considered to be of a different generation. More to the point, Ginny had been a toddler when Ashleigh's dreams had changed. She hadn't really been aware of Ashleigh as a person then, or her dreams and hopes. Ginny only knew of the Ashleigh who she had grown up with, not the Ashleigh who had wild notions of seeing other places and getting a degree in journalism. She hadn't known of the Ashleigh who had wanted to be *someone*, and do *something* with her life.

Ginny's eyes widened. "I had no idea about you wanting to travel, Ashleigh. I've never known about your dreams. *Ever.*"

"You wouldn't. It's only something I've been thinking about in recent years."

"In recent *years?*" Ginny cried, her expression one of pure astonishment. "What are you still doing here? Why haven't you gone?"

"How could I?"

"Easy. The way Eloise does, and I do. You've always been here for us and it's about time we repaid the favor and we were here taking care of things for you. Go. Go and follow your dreams. Why wait any longer?"

This was her chance. She lifted her glass and realized that it was empty. She refilled it again. Ginny had hardly touched hers. Tonight seemed to be a night of confession, of saying the things she'd been waiting to say. But it wasn't the wine that was making her throw caution to the wind. It was Ginny being an attentive listener that made her speak and not hold back.

"I was waiting until you got married. I've been looking at places I want to see, and I was trying to plan my trip, but it's all been vague and up in the air. We had so much going on with the wedding and then Eloise had Beth's bachelorette party and now she's at her wedding."

"She'll be back on Monday."

"I guess. I suppose I can tell you both then, when things settle down. I meant to, but something or other kept happening. I kept waiting and waiting for the right time to tell you. I didn't want to stress you out before your wedding, and then ... *that* happened. The Ben situation ... so ..." She let out a big exhale. "It never seemed to be the right time, but I was going to tell you both together, when Eloise returned."

"But then something else would probably have happened, and you would have had to wait even longer," Ginny said.

The truth of this hit Ashleigh hard, making her take notice. This was *exactly* what she did and how she dealt with things. She wasn't a get-up-and-go type of gal, she was a wait-it-out-and-see-what-the-signs-are-like-out-there type of person. She was always careful to not make too many ripples or upset too many people. The truth boomeranged back towards her, hitting her in the face, and she did something that took her by surprise.

She laughed.

It was a tiny laugh at first. "That *is* what I do, oh, my word. That is so what I do. I wait and wait and wait and wait." The laughter kept building, until she was soon hysterical with it. Ginny's eyes clouded over with worry, but Ashleigh kept on laughing and laughing until tears streamed down her eyes. And then she started to cry, wiping her tears away with her fingers.

"Ashleigh?" Ginny looked worried.

"I don't know why I'm crying," Ashleigh babbled in between sobs. The truth of Ginny's words had hit home. She had spent her life waiting until the time was right. But the time was never right. Life didn't always work out like that. Life didn't wait. If you wanted to do something, you had to jump right in and do it. If you needed something, you had to find it and claim it.

What you didn't do was wait for permission.

Waiting was for wimps.

It was the reason why she was where she was and why she felt the way she did; jaded and left behind, and irrelevant.

As if time and life had passed her by.

"The wine has gone to my head," she said, slowly composing herself. Especially when she saw the worry on Ginny's face. The last thing she wanted was to give Ginny something more to stress about. She fanned her face.

"It's too hot, and so much has happened." It was a lame attempt to explain herself. "And the wine didn't help."

"You should go."

"I think I should. It's getting late." But she couldn't move.

Couldn't get up off her chair because she felt a little dizzy. How much wine had she had? Two glasses were her absolute limit.

"Not to bed. I think you should go on your trip. I'm not getting married now, and Eloise and I can take care of things. You go, for as long as you need. Six months, a year—"

"Six months or a year?" Ashleigh shrieked. What planet was Ginny on? How could she take off for six months to a year? As it was, she'd been having kittens about going for two months.

"For as long as you want. You've taken care of us all your life, and it's about time we took care of you by letting you go and have some fun for a change."

Hearing her youngest sister say this to her made her feel all teary again and she was overcome with emotion. "You're so sweet, Ginny."

"That's because you raised me right."

And that almost sent her into tears again. Dear God. The wine was definitely making her go all mushy. It felt so good to be heard, to be understood, and the biggest shock was that the person doing the listening and the understanding was her youngest sister.

"Come on. Let me help you to bed." Ginny helped her to standing but even then Ashleigh had to take a moment. The room wasn't spinning, but she felt all light and fluttery as if her knees were boneless.

"Two months," Ashleigh stated.

"What?"

"Two months. I was thinking of going away for two months."

"Then make it happen. Do it."

"Do it?" Ashleigh scrubbed her cheek with her hand. Do it. Sure, as if it were that simple.

"It really is that simple."

"Did I say that out loud?" Ashleigh asked.

Ginny narrowed her eyes at her. "No, but you're so predictable, Ashleigh. I know what you're thinking."

Ginny cleared away the table and tidied up the kitchen as soon as Ashleigh had gone upstairs. Her sister had been harboring dreams of traveling and leaving the business for a few months.

How had she not known? Guilt washed over her like a thundering waterfall. She'd never really stopped to consider things from Ashleigh's point of view. And now she felt selfish for disregarding her sister.

At least Ashleigh had opened up to her now. If there was one thing Ginny was going to do, it was to make sure that Ashleigh's dream came true; it was such a small thing to wish for, and she would see to it that it came true.

CHAPTER 27

*S*he had her sister's blessing. Not that she had consciously been asking for it. Or had she? Yet Ginny knowing, and being fine about it, and telling her to go to Europe, had lifted a huge load off her mind.

She only needed to tell Eloise and then she could start getting ready. Ginny had been right. Ashleigh had played it safe for so long, had considered the thoughts and feelings of others before she had considered her own.

Now Ginny was telling her, almost giving her permission, making her feel as if it would be okay for her to go and do her own thing. Have some fun, travel, take some time to herself.

She wandered around the farmers' market carrying a bag full of vegetables in one hand, and a pound of guilt for leaving Ginny alone at home. But Ginny had insisted that she go out and do something. After her sun salutations on the yoga mat, she set off for a day wandering around the market, looking for fresh food and anything else that caught her eye.

Sunshine streamed down from above, warming her skin and making the whole world look brighter. Someone tapped her on the back.

"Fancy seeing you here." She recognized the voice, just before she turned around to stare into Ford's twinkling blue eyes. A quiver of shock and excitement pierced through her. Enough to make her jittery.

"Oh, hey," she touched her hair, tucked an imaginary lock behind her ear. "What are you doing here?"

He carried a big bag in one arm. "The same as you, from the looks of it."

"Vegetables, huh?"

Vegetables, huh? She cringed inside. What a thing to say. "This is the best place to get them."

They stared at one another, as the conversation came to an immediate stop. She tried to think of something to say, something safe, that wouldn't be about his past, or his ex, or his daughter, for fear of being too nosy. For fear of him thinking she was prying for more information. And yet it was difficult to remain nonchalant because Ford, divorced Ford, being back in Whisper Falls and talking to her, was the most exciting thing to have happened to her, personally.

"I heard about Ginny."

"News travels fast." She hated that this particular piece of news was making the rounds in Whisper Falls.

"You know it does. I'm sorry to hear what happened. How is she?"

"She's doing well, better than I expected." She had prepared herself for Ginny falling apart, maybe staying in bed for days, and sobbing, but she hadn't expected her to be as tough and as resilient as she seemed to be. She made small talk with Ford, telling him, without going into the details of what had happened, that life continued as usual, and that Ginny would be fine.

"How are *you* doing?" he asked, when an uneasy silence fell between them. Each time she looked into his eyes, she felt her guard slowly coming down. Ford Montgomery was a handsome man, and he seemed to get only more handsome with time. There was no denying the fact, and knowing that he was single again had somehow moved her 'ignore him' button from off to on.

Now he was staring at her. He'd asked her a question, but she had been too engrossed taking in the contours of his face, remembering the past again, that she didn't answer.

"Hey, Ash," he said, "How are you doing?"

"Who? Me?" She shook herself out of her reverie. "Oh, I'm okay. You know how it is. We're just being strong for Ginny."

"It must be hard when life throws a wrench like that in the way. You would know more than anyone. If there's anyone who can help Ginny through this, it's you."

Was he hinting at *their* situation all that time ago? Or was she reading more into it?

"This isn't like our situation was," she said quickly. "You're nothing like Ben."

"I'm not sure if that's a good thing or a bad thing. I feel completely ignorant."

"That's a good thing. It's a good thing, most definitely," she reassured him.

"Either way, a breakup is hard."

"Yes."

"I would have stayed here for you, if you'd wanted me to," he said, knocking the air clean out of her lungs as his words sank in.

"I know." It felt odd, him bringing that up now, after all this time.

"You're the one who told me not to wait for you."

"I didn't want you to give up your dream for me. I had no choice but to stay behind, but I didn't think it was fair to keep you stringing along."

"But I would have. You only had to say the word."

"You would have given up the job at your uncle's firm?"

"You know I would have. I could have gotten a job anywhere."

"You wouldn't have had the opportunities you did there. Darcie says you've got your own practice now."

"News does travel fast."

"We shouldn't revisit the past," she said, feeling a sting of regret burrow deep inside her. Talking about that time, about what might have been, was of no use now.

"It's been a long time since we talked, just you and me."

Her insides jangled, her nerves were on edge. The idea of Ford wanting to take a walk down memory lane made her anxious.

"I should get back. Ginny's in the shop alone and I don't want to leave her for too long."

CHAPTER 28

She didn't tell Ginny that she had run into Ford, but she couldn't help thinking about the way he had made her feel yesterday. Nervous and jittery. She needed to keep her distance; her heart behind a shield and her head level.

She also needed to tell someone. Darcie, specifically, and when she suggested she might meet her for lunch, Ginny asked her why she didn't meet her one evening for dinner instead.

"And leave you alone at home by yourself?"

"I'm a grown woman, Ashleigh. You don't have to babysit me, and you don't have to worry about anything else. I'm okay."

"I know you're okay. I like having dinner with you, that's all."

"Really? Because you see me at work all day, every day."

Talk about a punch to the stomach. She'd been enjoying her conversations with Ginny.

"I'm joking. Go meet Darcie one evening. Make an evening of it."

She could. She had many things to run by her friend. It had only been a few weeks since the big breakup and Ginny was soldiering on, which wasn't typical of her. Ashleigh was waiting for the fragile façade to crack and break. She felt sure it would eventually, and when it did, she wanted to be there to pick up the pieces.

"If you can't even go meet Darcie for dinner, how are you going to cope when you go abroad and leave us for months?"

"It's only going to be two months," said Ashleigh, putting her fork down.

"If you can't even leave me alone for an evening, you're going to struggle to leave the business for even one day."

Ashleigh picked up her fork again, and twirled more spaghetti on it, contemplating this.

"I'm grateful, and I'm sure Eloise is as well, that you've always been here taking care of us, but it's about time you stopped doing that, treating us like kids that you have to look after forever. Do you feel responsible for us even now?"

Ashleigh looked up, startled by this. "Of course I do. It's hard to let go."

"But we're not your kids. I mean ..." Ginny looked flustered. "We're not children."

"I know that."

"Did you ever want to have children?"

Why did Ginny ask such difficult questions? "I've never thought about it much." It had never been a yearning. Maybe when Darcie had been pregnant, she had wondered what it might have been like to have a child of her own, but with no long-term partner by her side, it hadn't been something she'd had to think about seriously.

"Never?"

"Not really."

"Because of Ford?" Ginny asked.

"Not because of Ford. He was out of the picture many years ago."

"And now?"

"Now?!" Whatever was Ginny talking about? "I'm forty-three. I'm too old to have them now."

"Women older than you have children."

"It's not something I want." When had Ginny turned into such a curious person?

"Why not?"

"I never wanted to have children because—" She didn't want to say it even though the words nearly tumbled from her mouth. Because she'd had her hands full bringing up Ginny from the age of two. Even though Aunt Becky had helped, it was Ashleigh that Ginny clung to in those initial early days when she couldn't find her mommy or daddy.

She'd had her fill of raising kids with Ginny.

That wasn't the only reason. There was also that other elephant in the room; she had never met a man she had felt the urge to grow old with. She'd never met someone she considered special enough or cared enough about to *want* to start a family with. When Darcie had met and married for the second time, and then started a family of her own, Ashleigh had been in Pity Street, feeling sorry for herself and wondering why things hadn't worked out for her but they had for Darcie. That had been a time of reflection for her, watching Darcie cradle her newborn, while she had looked on.

"It just wasn't for me," she said softly.

"Why not? You're so caring, Ashleigh. You have so much to give."

She swallowed, fighting the urge to tell her sister to stop pushing for answers and leave her be. She was so used to taking care of Ginny and being there for her, that she found this awkward, Ginny wanting to be there for her.

"It's not children that are in my future. It's the world. That's what I want. I want to go see some of the world."

Ginny beamed at her with joy. "Then that's what you must do."

"I'm working on it."

"Don't leave it too long."

Ashleigh picked up a glass of water and brought it to her lips. "I won't. I need to tell Eloise first."

"That won't take too long, telling Eloise. It's just words in a sentence. It should take you all of ten seconds."

Ashleigh blinked at her sister. Ginny talked as if it were that simple.

Later that evening, she brought out some of the travel brochures she'd been secretly hiding away out of her sisters' sight. She showed Ginny the places she planned to visit. The more she talked about her travels, the more enthused she became. It was no longer just a silent idea in her head. It was beginning to take shape and, in time, it was going to happen.

"You kept that quiet."

"I didn't get a chance to tell you, and I didn't want to tell you over the phone." She'd finished telling Darcie how she had run into Ford again at the farmers' market.

"Are you sure he's not stalking you?" Darcie asked as they walked along the seafront.

"Right?" Ashleigh cried. "I was beginning to wonder the same thing myself."

"First, he comes to visit you at the shop—"

"Saying he was just passing through," Ashleigh reminded her.

"Exactly."

"And then he runs into you at the market."

"And before that as well," said Ashleigh.

"Maybe he's missed you," Darcie suggested.

"We've had our own separate lives. All of that nonsense stopped the moment I came back. It did for me, I mean, we wrote to one another for a while, but that fizzled out, too."

"Why are you calling it nonsense? You had feelings for him, Ash. You were *crazy* about the guy."

Hearing it from Darcie's mouth, said like that, with Darcie-esque enthusiasm and intonation, reminded her of the tiny fact which she had tried to keep tamped down.

She had been, but bigger, more serious things prevented all the light and fluffy goodtime feelings. "But it stopped. I knew it wasn't going to turn into anything more. It couldn't. I didn't have the mental capacity for anything back then." But Ford had maintained that he would have come back to Whisper Falls if she'd asked. That had surprised her, the fact that he reminded her of that.

She couldn't deny it or pretend it wasn't there—that tiny hum of electricity, the sparks, the magic, the connectedness that still bound her to him, or felt like it did, all these years later. Perhaps it was no more than a harkening back to familiar times, this feeling that Ford had instilled in her, of life being an adventure, something they were both stepping into; a new journey they were going on together. There had been hope, and a sense of wonderment in the air, and as a young twenty-something, she had been more than ready.

But now, in her forties and jaded, life was so different. She felt resentment instead of exhilaration. Tedium instead of joy, in most things.

"He's single." Darcie pointed out, much to Ashleigh's annoyance.

"And?"

"And you're single too." Her friend really was a master at mentioning the obvious.

"And?"

"He's a handsome man. He's nice, he's not boring, and he's handsome. Did I already mention handsome?" Darcie cried. "He has his own hair, Ash. That's a huge bonus! Surely that has to count for something?"

"Stop it!"

Yes, Darcie had a point. Ford had taken great care of himself.

"Some lucky woman is going to snap him up if you don't."

"I have no intention of snapping him up," Ashleigh exclaimed, horrified at the thought. Though privately, her heart was thundering. These things had occurred to her, but there was no way she was going to act on anything.

"This is just like old times, you and me dissecting Ford and his words and actions like a pair of giggling teenagers," said Darcie.

"I don't know why I tell you anything."

But she did know. Because Darcie pointed out the obvious when Ashleigh chose to paint over it. She'd wanted to hear confirmation of the things she'd been thinking and feeling about Ford, and this Darcie had down.

There was so much truth in what Darcie had said that Ashleigh couldn't bring herself to look at her friend in the face.

CHAPTER 29

They walked into town together one lunchtime, leaving the assistants to tend to the shop. As they walked past the diner, Ashleigh saw Ford coming out of the diner and walking towards them. The familiar broad shoulders sent her insides into a tizzy. It seemed that wherever she went, she was suddenly seeing Ford everywhere.

He did a double take when he saw her, and then his gaze slipped to Ginny. He nodded, then stopped to talk, asking Ginny how she was. She told him she was fine, and they made polite small talk with Ginny deftly changing the subject and asking Ford how long he was on vacation here this time.

Ashleigh didn't like Ginny asking such a personal question, even though she was curious herself to know the answer.

"Who knows?" he answered rather cryptically. "I'm beginning to like it here. It's nice to be back. I'm not sure I want to return to Boston."

"Oh," said Ginny, and looked at Ashleigh, who wanted the ground to open up and swallow her. Like Eloise, Ginny didn't have much tact. "That's so strange, because Ashleigh is looking to get away from here."

"Get away?" Ford's blue eyes burned into her. "On a vacation, Ash?"

"I'm long due one," she answered. If she could have nudged Ginny in the ribs without Ford noticing, she would have.

"If anyone needs a vacation, it's you," replied Ford, completely oblivious to the tsunami of emotions he had unleashed inside her. "It would do you some good to get away as well," he said to Ginny.

"Oh, I'm not going. It's Ashleigh who's thinking of going around—"

"I just want a break," she said, interjecting before Ginny told Ford all of her life story.

"A break?" Ford's eyes filled with concern and an old familiarity returned. The times when he had looked at her like that didn't seem so long ago.

"It's so busy, running the bridal shop and it's been a while since I took time off. What are you doing here?" she asked, changing the subject quickly. "It seems that we keep running into one another."

"Darcie thinks I'm stalking you." He let out a light laugh.

"She said that?" Ashleigh's stomach almost bottomed out. She wondered when Ford and Darcie had been talking about her. She also didn't want Ford to think that she and Darcie had discussed him. They had, but he didn't need to know that they had. Girl talk was strictly girl talk.

Ford laughed, which made Ashleigh all the more curious as to what the two of them had been talking about.

"Ashleigh says your daughter is going to college in the fall?" Ginny remarked, promoting Ashleigh to wonder when the two of *them* had gotten so familiar.

"She is. I still can't believe it myself how fast she's grown. She's going off on her new adventure." His eyes caught Ashleigh's then, and she couldn't help but remember when she, too, had been ready to go off on her little adventure with Ford. Only, things had never gone according to plan at all.

She kept quiet while the conversation ping-ponged between Ford and Ginny. Ginny asked about what degree field his daughter was enrolling in, as if she and the daughter had been best friends. She couldn't wait to get her sister alone and give her a piece of her mind.

"We should get back." Ashleigh made an exaggerated motion of looking at her wristwatch. "We've been gone a while. Nice talking to you, Ford."

She hooked her arm in Ginny's and marched off. "Why were you talking to him as if the two of you were long-lost buddies?" she hissed.

"I know of him, and I was being polite. I've seen him in town a few times. Eloise always used to stop and talk to him."

"What?"

"I thought you knew?"

She didn't know. Eloise had known Ford, but Ashleigh had no idea that the two of them were even talking. Eloise had never mentioned it. "Why did you need to ask him what his daughter was doing?" She didn't want Ford to think that she was the one prying for all the information on him.

"I was being nice," Ginny threw back. "He couldn't stop looking at you, didn't you notice?"

No, she hadn't noticed, because she'd been too busy trying not to look at him. "Don't be so silly."

"I'm not. He couldn't."

"Do you know what your problem is, Ginny? You read too much into things."

"Well, I was trying to get us to spend more time with him, on account of you," Ginny retorted.

"You don't need to do anything on my behalf, especially when it comes to Ford Montgomery," Ashleigh huffed, walking back into the bridal shop.

It was hectic inside, and it had been growing steadily busy. One of the assistants came over and told them that they had a new customer who had been recommended to the store, and she was looking at dresses on the mannequins.

Ashleigh walked over and introduced herself.

"Helena sent me," the young woman told her.

Helena? Ashleigh tried to think. They met so many customers, and usually she was good with details, and names.

"Oh, Helena." She remembered. Helena and her entourage of family and friends who had come with her on her last fitting. Ashleigh chatted to the young woman and asked all about Helena's wedding, and the customer was happy to tell her in minute detail of the event and how impressed everyone had been with the bride's wedding dress.

"I'm looking for something like that, not exactly like that. I don't want to be accused of copying her, but something that has the 'WOW' factor."

"Don't worry. We'll find the perfect dress for you." Ashleigh smiled sweetly, and began the arduous task of discovering exactly what the bride-to-be wanted. She wished Eloise were here to do the job she was so good at.

A few hours later, Ashleigh had gone through some samples with the bride and had narrowed down the choice of dress to three different styles which the customer said she needed to sleep on and think about. "I love this place. Helena was so right," she gushed.

"Helena seems to know a lot of people who are getting married," Ashleigh replied, noting that they'd had a few people visit the shop after Helena's wedding.

"She has a large family, and lots of friends all of the same age. I can't tell you what a major jaw-dropping moment it was to see her walk in wearing that dress. It took all our breaths away. We had to know where she got it from."

"That's a great compliment." Ashleigh smiled warmly. "We like recommendations. Word of mouth is always the best recommendation."

"Thank you for your time. I'll think about everything we've talked about, and then I'll get back to you when I've decided which dress I want."

"Take all the time you need."

The customer turned to leave when something caught her eye. "Where dreams begin ... that's so beautiful," she enthused. "It's perfect."

"Thank you. I'm glad you like it."

"Helena said that someone was getting married?"

Ashleigh prayed that Ginny wasn't within hearing range. She winced and lowered her voice. "Unfortunately, things didn't work out. It didn't go ahead."

"It didn't?" The woman shrieked, louder than was necessary. From the corner of her eye, Ashleigh saw Ginny turn towards them.

"My sister would rather nobody talked about it."

"Of course, of course." The woman made a sorry face. "That's such awful news."

"It's been wonderful meeting you. Why don't you get back to me where you're ready?" Ashleigh tried to move the conversation along and hoped to encourage the customer to leave.

"I'll be in touch."

Ashleigh sucked in a breath and watched the customer leave.

"You can stop worrying about me, Ashleigh." Ginny walked over to the counter, looking morose. "I can handle it when people are being nosy. Most aren't even being gossips."

Ashleigh's heart sank. Ginny had heard her. "I know you can handle it. I'd just prefer it if you didn't have to hear it."

"People are curious, and a wedding being canceled is gossip. It's a story."

"People should mind their own business," Ashleigh grumbled.

"She didn't know. She was being polite," Ginny replied, being slightly more defensive than was necessary.

"Maybe it's not such a great idea, you being here just yet. As soon as Eloise returns, I think it would be a good idea for you to take some time off."

"Are you being serious? I'm not going to hide or go away, and you don't need to worry about me or protect me. I'm not fragile."

Ashleigh opened her mouth to protest. "I'm not saying you're fragile."

"I'm not being ungrateful. I just don't want you to fret about me. You always worry too much."

Ashleigh was about to say something but didn't, because if this week had taught her anything, it was that Ginny was usually right.

CHAPTER 30

*A*shleigh was in the kitchen cooking dinner when the phone rang and Ginny answered it.

She hoped it wasn't Ben. Every time the phone rang or there was a knock at the door, her insides fluttered like drunken butterflies at the thought that it might be him still trying to convince Ginny that he was the right man.

"You ate what?" Ginny asked, her eyes turning big and round. Ashleigh scowled as she carried the plates to the table and sat down. She listened to Ginny give all the right advice and say comforting words. It was him, and this was a new tactic. The little runt was sick and had the nerve to call Ginny in order to get some sympathy.

Ashleigh hoped her sister wouldn't go running over to check in on him. Then Ginny asked, "Do you want to talk to Ashleigh?" Her eyes nearly popped out of their sockets.

Ben? No, she did not want to talk to him.

Ginny spoke into the phone again. "Oh, okay. I'll tell her. Hope you get better soon." She hung up. Ashleigh's curiosity rocketed sky high.

"Why would I want to talk to him?"

"Him?" Ginny's brows pinched together as she sat down. "That was Eloise. She's got a bad case of food poisoning."

"What? What do you mean she's got food poisoning?"

"She ate some shrimp."

"And?"

"And she says she's not well enough to drive home yet."

"How bad is she? When did she get it? Why is this the first we've heard?" The questions tumbled out of Ashleigh's mouth. The wedding was last weekend and Eloise was supposed to drive back tomorrow evening.

Ginny made a face. "So many questions. Does it matter? She's sick. Let's hope she gets better soon. Food poisoning can't be nice."

She felt sheepish, having been chided gently by Ginny. "I hope she gets better, too." But she found it slightly odd that Eloise hadn't wanted to speak to her directly. "I should call her back and see how she is." Ashleigh stood up to reach for the phone.

"No, you don't," Ginny cautioned. "She's a grown woman. She's told me, and I've told you. She's not dying. She didn't even sound that bad, and she will be fine. She says she's going to see how she feels because the drive back will be tough. Sit down and eat, Ashleigh. You don't need to worry. You're not responsible for every little problem we encounter."

She shrugged and sat back down, at the same time wondering when Ginny had started dispensing advice and being in charge. Ginny went to the refrigerator and lifted out a jug of cold water with slices of lemon in it. She poured it out for both of them. After dinner, they went through some more of the travel brochures, only because Ginny had asked. She suddenly wasn't all that sorry that Eloise would be away for a little longer. She had enjoyed it being just her and Ginny.

The next day, when Eloise still hadn't contacted her, Ashleigh got worried and called her first thing in the morning.

At first Eloise didn't pick up, which made her even more worried, and then, just as she was about to hang up, Eloise picked up.

"Eloise? I've been so worried about you. What's this about the food poisoning?"

Eloise coughed. "It was … it wasn't too bad. Don't get so worried."

Hmmm. Eloise didn't sound too bad. In fact she didn't sound bad at all. She sounded really quite normal. "Ginny said it was something you ate."

"I think it was the shrimp. Beth's parents hosted a big party, every night has been a party, really, and it's been the most incredible atmosphere—"

"Haven't they left for their honeymoon yet?"

"They're going next week. They wanted to spend time with their family and friends, and you know that Beth's parents have a huge mansion—"

"Okay, I get the picture."

She felt cynical, but she didn't quite believe that Eloise was too sick to come home. Having too much fun seemed more like the issue.

"When do you think you'll be back?"

"I'll see how I feel. I'm not up to doing the long drive."

"Uh huh." Ashleigh sipped her coffee. "So we're not likely to see you this weekend?"

"I feel like death."

Ashleigh set down her cup. "Will we see you next week, do you think, or will this bug last for the entire month?" She couldn't help herself.

"You really don't believe me, do you?"

"I don't know what to believe." She bit her lip, wondering if she'd gone too far.

"I'll come home right now then!"

"I thought you said you didn't want to risk driving for hours?" Ashleigh retorted.

"I'm coming back. I'm going to drive back and if I have an accident—"

An abrupt silence mushroomed between them.

"You will stay put, Eloise." The pain of remembering turned Ashleigh's voice hoarse. "I'm sorry. I shouldn't have been so hard on you. You stay put, Eloise, and get well soon, okay?"

"Okay."

"Don't even think about driving until you are one hundred percent."

"Okay."

She hung up feeling ashamed of herself. She'd turned into the Vacation Police—watching and monitoring her sister's timeline and not believing her. She'd seen it throughout the years, through her customers; had seen the multi-generational results for herself. She'd witnessed first-hand how the young were so full of life and had a devil-may-care attitude, and how older people were more fixed in their ideas and viewpoints, reminiscing about 'the good old days' as if they'd been a golden era.

It wasn't Eloise's fault for wanting to have fun. Ginny walked in and poured her breakfast cereal into a bowl.

"That was Eloise," Ashleigh announced. "She's not coming home yet. It might be a few more days."

"Cool."

"And I'm going to see if Darcie's free tonight to meet up with me."

"Also cool."

CHAPTER 31

*S*he waited in line to be served, knowing exactly what she wanted to order, but as she quickly glanced around the diner, she found herself staring at Ford's weathered and smiling face.

"We meet again," he said, his voice low and even-tempered, with the magical ability to make her insides jump.

"We do." The way she said it came out grumpier than she had intended. Eloise being away hadn't improved her mood.

"Bad day?" Ford asked.

She sighed out loud then immediately regretted it. "Saturdays are always busy." She glanced up at the 'Specials' menu on the blackboard hanging above the counter, studying it carefully even though she was going to get the same sandwich she always did.

"Come and join me. I'm sitting over there." Ford pointed to a booth near the wall. "I won't bite, I promise."

Lunch, with Ford? Now? "Uh …"

"I'm hurt that it's taking you so long to decide." He placed a hand on his chest, feigning the pain.

Why not? "It's Saturday," she replied, looking for a way to get out of this. But Ginny was there and so were the assistants. Heck, there was nothing to stop her from agreeing to Ford's request, aside from the fact that having lunch with him would seem strange.

Strangely intimate, too.

"No wonder you need a break, if you can't even say a simple 'yes' to lunch."

She blinked at Ford. He was right. Ginny was right. "Fine, then. I'll have lunch here today."

"You'll join me?"

"You asked me, didn't you?"

"Yes, yes." He motioned for her to lead the way. There was a newspaper and glasses on one table.

"This one?" she asked, wondering when he'd started wearing glasses. He nodded.

They sat down across the table from one another and she was instantly transported back to another time, another place, another lifetime. This diner hadn't been here when they'd been dating, but there had been other such places and restaurants where they'd sat across the table staring at one another.

"This feels strange." Waves of nostalgia rolled over her, bringing back all sorts of memories. Memories of a time when Mom and Dad had been here, taking care of things. A time when she had been taken care of. She missed them so much.

"Strange?" Ford leaned forward, his tone full of concern, just like the look in his eyes. "It's just lunch, Ash. What are you worried about?"

"Nothing. It's … it's …" She tried to hold it together. It was too much, and too fast. She felt odd. Irritated by Eloise's phone call and now facing Ford, of all people. Sitting and having lunch with him when this was something she never did, least of all on a Saturday.

"Ash?" Ford looked genuinely worried and started to stand up. Oh, dear God. This was embarrassing. If this had happened in front of Darcie, it wouldn't be as big of a deal. Why now, in front of Ford?

"Don't," she said holding up her hand to halt him. She couldn't have him coming over to sit by her side, with his arm around her shoulder comforting her. Just like in the old days. "I'm sorry." She blinked a few times, hoping to dispel the tears she felt forming in her eyes. "I don't know what's come over me." Her emotions unleashing like this was going to become her downfall if she wasn't careful. She was supposed to be calm and in control. Together and composed. She was the one people went to for advice.

Ford didn't say a word, but seemed to be waiting for her to explain.

"It's just that ...uh ... it's been a strange time lately, and Eloise is away and things are hectic, and with Ginny's wedding being canceled, and ..."

"Is that why you're upset?" He didn't sound as if he believed her. She picked up the menu and looked up at him over it, using it as a shield, more than a menu, even though there was no need for her to consult it.

"It's a crazy time." She tried to inject some humor into her words, but when the corners of his lips only turned up a little, signaling empathy rather than the fact that he believed her, she knew she couldn't lie. She'd never been able to lie to Ford. He knew her and he always saw through her. She realized in that moment why she'd started to come apart—because with Ford, she could.

He understood her completely in a way no man had ever done. She'd dated, and gone out with men, always looking for her soulmate, the 'one' who would know her without the need for her to show or explain who she was. But she hadn't found anyone like that again, ever.

Meeting Ford first, then losing him had made her subsequent

romances hard to live up to. Ford had been the one for her and she'd never found a man who had come close to him. The realization slapped her in the face like a wet towel, leaving a dull pain and a lingering sting.

After her parents' accident, she'd never been the same again. She hadn't looked for men who could wine and dine her and show her a good time, or men who could make her laugh, though that certainly helped. She'd looked for someone who would see into her broken heart, someone who would have the compassion and understanding to help her to mend, but her quest had been futile.

And now the love of her life was back in town.

"I can imagine it's been tough for you all. But, knowing what you're like, I imagine you've been your usual self and tried to hold everyone and everything together."

"It's ... it's a lot of things. I don't even know if I can pinpoint it down to just one thing."

"It's obviously taking its toll on you. You're the same as ever, Ash. Taking care of everyone else and forgetting to take care of yourself."

His words cushioned her and were like soft silk to the hardness she'd put up around her. "I'm sorry for boring you with all of this."

"You're not boring me. I'm just glad you're here and we're talking again. It feels like ..."

She looked at him. "It feels like?"

His lips twisted, as if he wasn't sure.

"I won't bite you. Just say it," she urged him.

"It feels like old times, you and me, sitting and talking together, waiting to be served."

She nodded, because it really did. The iron armor in which she'd encased herself was in danger of becoming undone. "We should order," she said, forcing an upbeat tone. She sat upright and looked around for a server. "I don't have long, and this is a rare treat for me, having lunch away from the shop."

"Then I'm a very lucky man." The corners of his lips tugged upwards and she couldn't help but reflect a smile back. If they kept the topic of conversation on neutral safe subjects, this would be okay.

They ordered food, and over a lazy, long lunch talked about things in their past, general things, not about them, but about family. He talked about his daughter, while she told him more about life at the bridal shop, and about Ginny who seemed to be coping so much better than she'd thought she would.

"It must be a Rose trait," he answered.

She stared at him blankly. "A Rose trait?"

"You women are so strong and resilient. You especially. You rebounded after your parents' accident, Ash. Your strength was made from steel. I don't know where it came from."

"I had to be strong. I had to take care of my sisters."

"I was heartbroken for you. We all were, you know that."

She had never forgotten how the community had rallied around, how neighbors and friends and so many people had come out of nowhere and brought food every night for almost a month, maybe longer. Aunt Becky had been overwhelmed by the help and support of 'the good folks of Whisper Falls' each time she set down another tray of food that someone had brought them.

"You were my hero."

"Your hero?"

"Heroine," he said, correcting himself.

She wasn't questioning his use of the word, but was speechless at what he had said.

"You were. Everyone was astonished. My parents, friends, everyone in the community, Ash. You didn't see it or know about it, because you were so buried in your grief."

"I was trying to keep things sane for Eloise and Ginny. I don't know what I would have done without Aunt Becky. Bless her soul." She glanced upwards.

"I've always admired your courage. You just carry on, stoic, in the face of adversity."

"I didn't have a choice. Being busy was a way to avoid the pain of what had happened. It meant I could push it away and think about it later, when things had calmed down." She stopped, the thought coming to her that this was exactly how Ginny was behaving.

"I tried to be there for you."

"You *were*." Ford had been a great comfort to her, and maybe she had been too consumed by her grief to tell him them. "You were there for me, Ford. I knew that no matter what, I could count on you."

"I would have stayed."

"But I didn't want you to." She stared into his eyes, curious as to why he was bringing this up again so soon when they'd discussed this very thing a few days ago. "We don't have to keep talking about that time, Ford."

"We've never really talked about it."

"Do we have to?" She sensed a determination in his tone that hadn't been there before.

"Should we choose to ignore it?"

She opened her mouth to tell him that 'yes,' they should, but while this had been easy to do when he had been married, she sensed an urgency behind his need now. Maybe it was closure that he was after.

She'd still kept his letters to her from before the split. Every once in a while, when she was feeling down, she would read them. Maybe there was a need to say the things they hadn't and to put a seal on their past.

"What is there to say? What do you want to say?"

"You pushed me away, Ash. I was prepared to stay here for

six months. We weren't going to travel so I could have stayed—"

"I couldn't let you do that."

"It wasn't your decision to make. I wasn't going to go traveling by myself, and I was prepared to stay here with you for those months, but you didn't even want me here."

With their traveling plans abandoned, she'd told him to go to Boston and start working with his uncle sooner, but he had wanted to stay with her during that time. She knew that she would never leave this town, and she had said some nasty things to him. She was angry, bitter and frustrated, while he had been trying to help and support her, but she didn't want it on her conscience that he'd forgone his chance to leave Whisper Falls and go to the city where he had a good chance to make a life and build a career.

The server passed by asking them if they everything was okay and whether they wanted anything else. They looked at one another and shook their heads, with Ford answering that he couldn't have asked for anything more, because this was perfect. There was something in his expression which she couldn't read.

She couldn't help but remember the past and their happier days; the scent of summer, and new dreams and adventures yet to be taken. These last few weeks of seeing him so often was weakening her defenses.

They continued to talk, and she asked about Boston and his business there, questions which he happily answered. He told her that he'd needed to take some time away after his divorce. He didn't talk about his wife, nor his marriage much at all. "And with mom being sick, even if she hadn't been, I found myself wanting to come back home. Home is always the place we return to."

"From the city?" She cocked her head, not understanding the appeal of Whisper Falls compared to life in a big city. She had assumed that Boston was the place that he would call home now.

"How long will you stay?" she asked, then immediately

regretted it. She didn't want him to think that she was digging for information, and worse—that she cared.

"I'm not sure. Sometimes I feel like I don't ever want to leave." His blue eyes twinkled just as a tiny rush of air escaped from her lungs.

"Never leave? But don't you feel hemmed in, coming back here, especially after Boston?"

"I love it here, and I'm not so sure I want to go back."

This was new. "Really?" Her insides fluttered with hope.

"There's nothing for me there now. And my mom is getting frail and isn't so well."

"Please tell your mom I said 'hi.' I'm sorry to hear that she's not well." She liked Ford's mom. His parents had been good to her and had been so supportive after her parents had passed.

"I will. She was asking about you."

"Oh?" In what context would his mother have asked about her?

He gave a little chuckle. "Maddie mentioned that we'd run into you."

"She did, did she?" Now she was really curious. But before she could think of a way to get him to reveal more, he made an announcement that she wasn't expecting.

"I could start a small practice here."

"In Whisper Falls?"

"Home. This is home to me, and it feels more like home than ever before."

She peered at him not understanding. It was hard to comprehend this given the fact that he'd been gone for so long, had started a life and a family elsewhere, but still deemed this as ' home.'

"I don't need to be making lots of money. We have, *I* have— now that we've split everything between us—I have enough that I don't need to worry about retirement, but I need to have *something* to do. I'm not the retiring kind. I'm not old enough to wake up and want to do nothing."

"I know the feeling. I'm sometimes overwhelmed, especially when we get so busy over the summer, and things turn hectic. I ask myself why I'm doing this, but then I know, I would miss it if I didn't."

The revelation was huge, even as she said it. "I'm so used to being busy, that I don't know what I'd do if I didn't have something to keep me occupied." Jetting off around the world, or Europe at the very least, was an adventure of epic proportions, but after a few months, she had a feeling she would be ready to come back. Maybe not to the bridal shop—though that was a matter she would have to bring up and discuss with her siblings—but sitting idle from now to her mid-sixties and beyond wasn't an option. She needed something to keep her busy.

"And that's why you're taking a vacation?"

"I desperately need one."

"You always were a workaholic."

"Can't sit still, my mom always used to say."

Ford laughed. "She did. She used to say I was doing a great thing by whisking you away – her words not mine."

"My mom was so happy for us. She thought it was a wonderful thing, us traveling and seeing the world. I know it's what she wanted to do in her later years."

Her breaths stilled in her chest. A lump caught in her throat and held there. Her mother's memory never left her, nor her father's, but it was her mother who she'd confided in and shared her dreams with, of Ford, and their future plans, and it was her mother who had sat with her talking about their trip, and her journalism degree. She'd been so excited for her. "I can't wait to hear what it's like, Ashleigh," she'd said.

And that was the kicker; the real punch in the stomach that permanently winded her each time she thought back to when she'd heard the traumatic and life-changing news of the accident. Her mother never would get to hear about it. None of it, ever, about each of their lives. That was the heartache Ashleigh could never mend. She tried to suppress the sob that felt ready to burst from her chest, but she somehow managed to put on a brave face. Being around Ford turned her bones and muscles soft and squishy and made her grittiness crumble to dust.

"Hey, Ash?" His soft voice brought her back to the present.

"I'm okay, I'm okay." But a tear rolled down her cheek, and she hastily wiped it away. Too late. He'd seen it and scooted over to her side, putting his arm around her shoulder, just like he used to in the olden days.

"I don't know what's come over me. Sorry."

He pressed her arm gently, the feel of his big, weighty hand bringing back memories that made her insides warm and fuzzy. But just when she was getting used to it, his warmth and his hard protectiveness, he moved away to sit back opposite her. She felt the cold emptiness in the space he had vacated.

"Eloise has food poisoning," she announced, finding a safer topic to discuss, and then proceeded to tell him about Eloise.

They talked for a long time. Easygoing conversation, safe, and light, and ending too soon.

"This was nice," he said, as they got ready to leave.

She nodded. It was the nicest lunch she'd had in a while, and when she looked at her watch, and saw that more than two hours had passed, she let out a yelp.

"What's wrong?"

"The time. I didn't realize we'd been sitting here for so long."

"I'm glad you came here today, Ash."

"I'm glad you noticed me enough to come over," she replied.

"I always notice you. You're hard to miss."

She pressed her lips together because she didn't know what to say to him. She had lots of things she wanted to say, and talk about, now that the gates had been opened. And now that she'd spent a few hours in his company, with just the two of them, she realized just how much she had missed him.

"Darcie told me you liked to go for a walk into town, and that sometimes you get your lunch from here."

"Is that why you're always here?" she asked cheekily.

"I wouldn't say always. I need to eat, and their food is pretty darn great, but knowing that you come here is a pretty good incentive."

She pretended to be outraged. "You *are* stalking me."

"I'm taking time away from work, taking care of other matters, and I don't have anything better to do. Seeing you, though, it brings back all kinds of memories, Ash. I wanted to talk to you, but each time we ran into each other outside, you always seemed in a rush to get away."

"I'm busy."

"I can see. That's why I rushed over as soon as you walked in. I just want to be friends again, Ash. I've missed my friend."

She stared at him in the new safe space. She was scared of getting reeled into to his charm again. It had been easy to block him out of her mind as soon as she'd heard he was married, but now, with him returning to Whisper Falls, divorced, no less, it helped take her guard down. Seeing him that first day when he'd walked into the shop, it had brought it all back; her twenty-one-year-old self, and the dreams and ambitions she'd had back then. She had wrestled over thinking about him, but they kept running into one another and that didn't help.

And now he wanted to be her friend.

She could do that.

She could be his friend.

She would very much like to be his friend.

They'd shared a life before, a happy life full of possibility. Just being around Ford now was enough to give her a reminder of that time.

She needed a solid, firm friend like Ford. She already had Darcie, but Ford promised a hint of newness, a reminder of old times, and the exact amount of excitement that she needed to spice up her otherwise Groundhog Day existence.

"I'd like that," she said.

CHAPTER 32

"*I*'m back!"

Eloise's voice floated over to them from the hallway. Ashleigh and Ginny were having dinner and Ginny got up and went to greet her. Ashleigh stayed put, listening to the excited banter as she continued to eat her dinner, pretending to be completely engrossed in her food. Silent fury raged inside her. Eloise had returned a week later than planned.

A stony silence chilled the air as Eloise stepped into view.

"You're back at last," Ashleigh said, trying and failing miserably to sound happy.

"If I could have stayed away, I would have." Eloise was back and feeling crabby. Fun times.

"How are you feeling?" she asked, almost as an afterthought, because her sister looked and sounded completely fine from what she could see.

"I'm better today."

"Better today?" Ashleigh raised an eyebrow. Eloise sounded completely fine. Her normal self. No hint of post-illness recovery. She was surprised that Eloise had returned today, instead of taking the entire weekend off.

"Did you want to eat with us?" Ginny asked, sounding over-the-top cheery.

Eloise glanced at their food plates then turned her nose up. "I don't feel like eating. It was a long drive. *Looooong.* I stopped a couple of times along the way and had something. I need to get some sleep." Eloise yawned as if for added effect.

"Then you'd better get to bed so that you can get to the shop early," Ashleigh said.

Eloise yawned again. "Wonderful. I'm so lucky to be back."

The sarcasm wasn't lost on Ashleigh. "You've got a lot of consultations lined up tomorrow."

"Even better." Eloise rose to standing. "Thanks for that. It's exactly the type of welcome I expected from you."

"Aren't you going to tell us about the wedding?" Ginny asked. Ashleigh had held off from wedding talk until the time when Ginny wasn't around.

"Not now. I'm tired. 'Nite." Eloise went upstairs.

"Did you have to say that?" Ginny grumbled.

"Say what?"

"Talk about work and remind her that she's got to be there. She knows she has to, that's why she's come back today."

Ashleigh winced, feeling sheepish. "Did I seem really rude?" She'd tried to mask her anger.

"What do you think? You're always mad at Eloise. It's as if you hate the fact that she's had fun and been away. It's like you resent her doing anything but work."

"That's not true." But even as she denied it, she knew Ginny was right.

"You sound like you do. She's been driving for hours. You could have been nicer."

A wave of guilt rolled over Ashleigh as she raked a hand through her hair. She was turning into a monster and what Ginny

176

had accused her of was true; she did resent Eloise having fun, having a life and doing fun things.

"You didn't even ask her about the wedding. You didn't ask her anything about the food poisoning."

"That's because she looked fine to me—"

"You don't even think she was sick, do you?" Ginny hissed, looking over her shoulder as if she feared Eloise was there. Ashleigh set down her cutlery and slumped back in her chair.

"Okay, enough already. I hear you. You've made me feel like a teacher interrogating a juvenile delinquent."

"That's because you might as well be."

"Oh, my word." Ashleigh buried her face in her hands as she tried to recall the conversation from her sister's point of view. Knowing that Eloise had been driving for hours, and was probably tired, and maybe convalescing too, she could have given her a warmer welcome. Though taking an entire week off for a food bug didn't seem right.

"I think you going away will be good for you, and for everyone else."

Ashleigh looked up, startled by her sister's words.

"She's back now, so you have to make sure and tell her—"

"Tell me what?" Eloise stepped into view.

"Have you been hovering around the door eavesdropping the entire time?" Ashleigh asked.

"I came downstairs to get my luggage and you were both whispering. What do you have to tell me?" Eloise demanded.

"Not now," Ashleigh mumbled. It was too late in the evening to be talking about her plans, and the atmosphere was still icy. It would be far better to drop this bombshell once things had calmed down between them both.

"Well, what is it?" Eloise asked again. Ashleigh found Ginny staring at her with large eyes, urging her to say something.

"It can wait until tomorrow," Ashleigh insisted, not wanting to discuss her travel plans now, with Eloise being in a sulky mood.

"Just tell her," Ginny said. But now wasn't the time to announce her plans to Eloise.

"Not now, Ginny."

"Not now what?" Eloise's expression turned stormy. "Are you sick?" Eloise moved towards her. "What is it, Ash?"

Ashleigh softened at the worry in her sister's voice. "I'm not sick. It's not that at all."

"Then wh—"

"Ashleigh wants a break, and she's taking a few months off from the business."

"What?" Eloise cried. "Take a few *months* off? What in the world for?"

Ashleigh glared at Ginny. Why in the world did she have to go and open her mouth now?

"For a break," Ginny replied.

"For a break?" Eloise's eyes widened in shock. "And what about us?"

"What about us?" Ginny said quietly. She seemed caught off guard by Eloise's response, but Ashleigh wasn't. This was exactly what she'd expected from her. "We'll manage."

"For months? How many months exactly?"

"I don't know yet," Ashleigh answered. It was too darn late to be having this argument.

"It had better not be too long. Months, did you say?"

Ashleigh turned to her sister with a smug expression. "Ginny said I should go for six."

"Six?" Eloise shrieked, her eyes narrowing to slits. "Half. A. Year? Is this about reliving the trip you and Ford were supposed to go on?"

"It has nothing to do with that." Now she was doubly pissed, not only by Eloise's reaction which, as prepared as she had been for it, she just hadn't wanted to deal with it now. Mentioning Ford and that trip added more fuel to the fire. "I don't understand why you're so mad about it. It's just a suggestion so far—"

"No. It's something you're going to do," Ginny interjected.

"I don't want to talk about it now. I wish you hadn't brought this up now," she said to Ginny.

"Then it's a good thing I overheard you."

"You were away, on vacation."

"I was sick!"

"That, too," said Ashleigh, not caring that her voice had a don't-give-a-damn tone about it.

"I'm taking tomorrow off," she announced. "I wasn't going to, on account of it being so busy, and you not being well, but you're here now, so I'm taking my day."

Ginny started to clear the dishes away. "As you should."

"It's so great to be back!" Eloise yelled, opening the fridge door and grabbing a juice carton before slamming it hard.

"I can't deal with this drama."

"It's going to be fine. You're tired, and Eloise is exhausted from the drive." Ginny tried to assure them both. "It will work out."

Ashleigh wasn't so sure and she felt like the bad cop as she trudged up the stairs. This wasn't how she wanted to be; old, fed up and frustrated. She was in danger of going into middle age and turning into a crabby and unhappy woman, easily prone to being judgmental and worse. She didn't want to be that person.

CHAPTER 33

*E*loise wasn't happy. She hadn't been enthused about coming back and would have gladly stayed for the weekend, but she knew Ashleigh would be miserable if she did.

While she had braced herself for Ashleigh being pissed with the extra week she'd had off, Eloise hadn't expected Ashleigh to be making plans about taking months away from the business.

Months.

If she'd had any idea of the kind of reception she'd have, she would have gladly stayed at Hyannis Port even longer, and this time without making up a reason for it. She hadn't been sick the entire time, she hadn't even been *that* sick and while she'd felt guilty for lying to her family, it was the only way she'd been able to spend more time in Hyannis Port.

Meeting a friend of Beth's new husband had been reason enough for her to enjoy her vacation even more. After all, who in their right mind would want to come back to the hassle and headache of the shop?

Besides, it wasn't as if Whisper Falls had a great selection of available bachelors.

"When did she tell you this?" Eloise demanded, as she drove

both her and Ginny to the shop. Ashleigh hadn't even woken up and come downstairs, like she usually did on her days off. Eloise suspected that her sister was probably staying out of sight in order to avoid a confrontation.

Unfortunately, Ashleigh was becoming more miserable the older she got. She hadn't even asked about Beth's wedding, or the food poisoning. She'd been moody from the moment Eloise had returned.

The freedom of her vacation, of not being chained to the shop floor, of being away from home and her sisters, and having fun— that freedom was hard to let go of. This lifestyle clearly wasn't working. It had once, out of necessity. She understood the sacrifices Ashleigh had made in order for them to stay together, and for their parents' business to prosper. And while she had never been happier to have a home to come back to, after her short-lived marriage had failed, now they were in each other's faces. Working and living together wasn't as great as it used to be.

The customers were lovely, the business was a thriving success, but she didn't want to be tied to it all her life. She wanted to *have* a life. And The Bridal Shop wasn't the type of life she had in mind.

"You'll have to ask her," Ginny said, looking out of the window. Eloise stole a good look at her sister's face, trying to gauge how she was and how she had been handling the trauma of discovering that her fiancé might have cheated. Add to that the stress of a wedding that had been hastily canceled, it was Ginny who needed the break, not Ashleigh. "How are you doing, Gin?"

Ginny turned to her. "Me? You don't have to worry about me. I'm doing great."

The way she said it, the bravado, the nonchalance, told her that Ginny wasn't doing as well as she liked to make out.

"Did Ash give you any time off while I was away, or did she get her whip out and make you work just because I was away?"

Ginny frowned as if she didn't understand the question. "I wish you two would stop sniping at each other. We've been really busy. Being at the shop was the best place for me. It stopped me from sitting around and having nothing to do but think about … stuff."

Stuff. Ben. His probable cheating. A wedding canceled. Big life stuff. She was so caught up in her own plans and what Ashleigh's travel plans might mean for her that she'd forgotten that Ginny was the one who needed to be taken care of. "It probably was the best thing for you, Gin." She felt like an idiot. "How are you dealing with things? Are you eating? Sleeping?"

"Ashleigh's been taking really good care of me. We've been spending a lot of time together, now that I don't have …" She stared at the floor momentarily, lost in a thought. "Talia and the girls have been good. Real good."

"Yeah?"

"They've kept me distracted, but it's also been nice to just go home after a busy day, and have dinner with Ashleigh. Crack open a bottle of wine and talk about things."

Eloise nodded. "Good. You've been busy, huh?"

"We've had some customers come through from Helena's wedding. Do you remember her? I wanted my buttons to be like her satin ones."

"I remember." Eloise remained quiet and waited for Ginny to elaborate, but for the duration of the car ride, her sister didn't say another word.

Inside the shop, it all came back. The smell, the feel, the pressure—to deliver the best for the most important day in the life of a woman. *One* of the most important days. Soon, the shop would be full of customers. She hadn't minded it once. In fact, she'd loved it, but all the good things and positives about having a family business had started to fade.

If she'd been working for someone else, and she got bored

and fed up, she would have started looking for work elsewhere. If she'd become disenchanted and disillusioned about her day-to-day tasks, and fed up with the customers, or her colleagues or her boss, she would have left.

It wasn't so easy with a family business.

Something would have to change, and soon. Being away at the wedding had given her plenty of time to think about her future.

"I'll let you catch up with your emails," offered Ginny, "I'll go onto the floor."

"Thanks. I'll try to get through the backlog quickly." She didn't want to look through the orders book, or check the alterations that needed to be made to various dresses, but most of all, she dreaded seeing how many consultations she had lined up for today.

Being back was worse than she had imagined, and she'd tried not to think about it. Speaking to Ashleigh on the phone, trying to explain how sick she was, when she wasn't so bad, lying about it, hadn't been easy.

But, as soon as the customers started to come into the shop, she swung back into fully operational mode. Time flew. She survived the day, but was extremely exhausted. If Ashleigh had had a heart, or cared, she would have let Eloise come to work later, or even take the day off.

Working all day after driving all that distance yesterday made her bone tired. She wandered into the store room at the end of the day, and started putting things away.

"What's this?" She knocked on the top of a large, ornate wedding dress box. "It doesn't have a label."

"That's because it doesn't belong to anyone." Ginny hooked her fingers into the belt loops of her pants as she leaned against the wall.

Eloise lifted the lid and peered inside, slowly lifting out part of the dress. In the next instant she recognized that it was Ginny's.

"Oh, Gin."

"I'm sending it back. I don't want to sell it in the shop. I don't want to know who buys it. I know we won't get as much for it, what with the fittings and the alterations—"

"Don't worry about any of that. It doesn't matter."

"I'm sorry. I would rather we'd send it back. I feel sick in my stomach just looking at it."

"Oh, hon. Come here." She walked over to give Ginny the biggest hug. "It's probably the best place for it, sending it back to where it came from."

"I don't want it in the shop," Ginny whispered. Eloise pushed the box right up against the wall, then stuck a note on it, to remind her what it was. She would see to it that it was returned. "Don't worry about a thing. I'll take care of it."

"Ashleigh was going to."

"Then why hasn't she?"

"We've been really busy."

"Today wasn't *too* busy. We've had busier days. I wish Ashleigh would stop making a big deal about these things."

"Don't be so hard on her."

Ginny seemed to be Team Ashleigh all of a sudden. "I appreciate that you and Ash have undergone some sort of bonding experience, but you saw how she was last night."

"She's tired. You've been gone almost two weeks."

Eloise sighed loudly. "I know. It just didn't seem that long. Time flew by. It was ... it was just so much fun."

"Being sick was fun?"

Eloise coughed. "No. I was throwing up and I had cramps."

"You poor thing."

A sliver of guilt slid over Eloise. She'd thrown up and had cramps on the first day, and she had eaten something that made her stomach queasy, but she hadn't been sick the entire time. She'd been dehydrated and listless the next day, but that was all. It was a good thing she had someone taking care of her.

She could have returned a few days earlier, but she'd had so much fun. And she'd felt a connection she hadn't had in a while. "But it was also nice to have a complete break from the shop."

"That's how Ashleigh feels. She needs to get away."

"For months?" Eloise cried.

"She's never had many breaks. Not like you."

"Great, now she's poisoned you against me, too."

"Stop it. Just stop and think about it. Think about all the things Ashleigh has done and all the times she's been here for us. I know you've both been here for me, but think about how many times she steps in for us and we take her for granted."

Eloise stared at the floor. A part of her had felt guilty about lying and having those extra days off. It hadn't completely skipped her mind that while she had been partying in Hyannis Port with someone tall, dark and handsome, Ashleigh had been toiling in the shop, with one woman down, and that Ginny was still getting over the split with Ben.

It had been selfish of her to do what she had done, but sometimes, being selfish was necessary.

She now felt better, more refreshed, and happier than she had in a long time.

But as for the future, a new love. It was so fragile. She didn't know if there was a future.

"Can't you see how unhappy Ash has been lately?"

"Lately?" Eloise scoffed. "Ash has been premenstrual for months." She stopped. "I wonder if that's the reason why she's been so moody? She's perimenopausal, not premenstrual."

"What?"

"I wonder if she's going through menopause."

Ginny let out an exhale. "She's too young for that."

"She's in her early forties. It can start now."

"I don't think it's that. She just needs time away. She gave everything up for us."

"Anyone would have done what she did," Eloise retorted.

Ginny's face turned red, her eyes blazing with anger. "Why are you always so ungrateful?"

"I'm not. I'm just saying, Ash isn't a saint."

"She's not the evil witch you make her out to be either."

"Oh, my goodness," Eloise groaned in a low voice, hearing the words coming out of her mouth. She leaned against the wall. She'd had her fun and adventure, and maybe there was more to come, but Ashleigh never did. She couldn't remember the last time her sister had dated and been truly happy. Single, in her forties, and tied to the shop, her sister never ventured too far out of Whisper Falls. Unlike Eloise, Ashleigh had no college friends out of state that she could visit and do girlie trips with. Darcie was her best friend. And unlike her, Ashleigh had never married and tasted some of that life. "I do sound like an ungrateful cow, don't I?"

Ginny nodded her head, a little too eagerly. "Yes."

"Thanks."

"You're welcome."

CHAPTER 34

By the time Ashleigh came downstairs for breakfast, her sisters had already left.

She felt restless and unrested having gone to bed but unable to sleep. The confrontation with Eloise had played heavily on her mind. She blamed herself for it, for not believing that her sister had been so sick, and she was determined to make it up to her this evening. She hadn't wanted Eloise to find out about her future plans the way she had. She'd wanted more time to prepare her. Ginny had done her no favors spouting off the way she had.

She got up and showered, and had the sudden urge to see Ford, because he would understand. Darcie would, too, but Ashleigh didn't want to interrupt her friend during the weekend if she could help it. Besides, her insides fluttered at the idea of seeing Ford again.

Knowing that he liked to frequent the diner, she went there to have her breakfast. She wanted to treat herself and do something different, as well as get out of the house in order to have a good think about this evening, when Ginny and Eloise would be home for dinner.

She walked into the diner and glanced around casually,

wondering if by any miracle Ford might be in here. Instead, she almost walked right into him.

"Ash?" Her heart danced at the sound of his voice, but the dancing soon stopped when she saw that he was with his daughter.

"Hi." She acknowledged them both. "I'm here for breakfast," she stated, then gave herself a mental kick. Why would he want to know what she was doing here?

"That's a shame. We were just leaving."

"I feel like blueberry pancakes," she managed to say.

Maddie gave her a weak uninterested smile. "Dad, I'll meet you outside." She was clearly unable to take this stilted, boring adult conversation any longer.

I feel like blueberry pancakes? Dear God. Had she really gone and said that?

Ford's eyes twinkled with amusement. "They're good, but not as good as the ones you used to make."

"You liked them," she said, wondering if he had intentionally waited for his daughter to leave before he said it. Then she wondered why he'd said it at all.

"You know I did." He scratched his ear. "Well, uh, enjoy your breakfast." But he didn't move. Now she wished she'd come here earlier, but given the fact that he'd been with his daughter, there was no way she would have joined them, even if he'd asked her to.

"Thanks. You too. I mean, enjoy the day, because you've already had your breakfast."

She cringed inside and wished she could spontaneously evaporate. She had the unenviable skill of saying the most banal things whenever this man was around.

"Maddie needs sportswear. Her mom used to take care of these things before. Maddie's old enough to buy it herself, but you know kids these days, they want their parents to pay ..." His expression turned apologetic. "Sorry."

"Don't be." Talk of kids, and marriage, and the things she didn't have; he didn't need to apologize for that. "I'd better go order some of those blueberry pancakes." She turned to go. "You have a good day."

"You too. I was going to go to the farmers' market later," he mentioned, casually brushing his hand through his hair.

"Nice day for it. I had plans to go there later, or maybe tomorrow. It's my day off today so maybe I'll wander over there later." Even as her mouth continued to move of its own accord, she had the sinking feeling that this was too much information and that he probably didn't care what she did and when she did it.

But then again, he was the one who'd mentioned that he'd be at the farmers' market, and he hadn't needed to reveal that.

Maybe this wasn't so one-sided after all? Maybe Ford liked her company, too?

"Well, maybe I'll see you there later?" He fixed her with a lingering gaze that caused ripples of anticipation in her belly. It was all coming back now, his looks, his mannerisms, his ways. The things she had erased from her mind were slowly being painted back in.

She sat down to order her pancakes, and even though her stomach was empty, her heart was already full. She didn't need a lot to lift her mood. Just the small things.

Why had he told her that he'd be going to the farmers' market later today? It had been a blatant invite to Ashleigh. Blatant.

Ford walked away from the diner wondering what the heck had just happened. He had stopped thinking about Ashleigh Rose when he'd met Susan. But although he had stopped thinking about her, he never forgot her, and now they seemed to be running into one another a lot—which wasn't a bad thing.

He'd forgotten what it was like to look into those hazel eyes. Memories flooded back, of a past that seemed so much longer than it really was. He'd lived and loved a lifetime between then and now. He'd loved Susan, but things between them splintered long before she had suggested they sleep in separate bedrooms.

Now that he was back in his home town, he saw Ashleigh everywhere, if not physically, then in his mind's eye. He hadn't come to Whisper Falls wanting anything; he'd had no expectations, nothing. He'd wanted space and a break from Boston, before deciding on the next chapter in his life, one which involved taking care of his mother, but also taking care of *himself*.

Maddie would be fine, starting a new life at college, and Susan was married to her career. He wasn't so sure that he would be returning to Boston anytime soon because there was a lot to keep him here.

She felt like a young girl, going to the farmers' market on the pretense of shopping but with her eyes scanning the market stalls and people gathered around them, she was looking for a glimpse of Ford.

It was pathetic. She told herself that she needed vegetables and the freshest produce, and that's why she was here, but it wasn't the truth. She knew it, and so would Ford, if she chanced upon him here.

It was when she felt a gentle touch on her shoulder that she sheepishly turned around, already knowing. She found herself a little too excited, a little too happy, a little too dizzy as she stared into his twinkling eyes.

"Hey." She hadn't expected him to already be here. She'd had her breakfast and had come right over, and running into one another so soon was a little embarrassing.

"It would make more sense if we'd come here together," he said, before hurriedly adding, "as friends."

"Weren't you shopping with your daughter?"

"I was. I did."

They started to walk, even though neither had asked whether they wanted to go around together.

"It's my day off," she explained. "I needed to get out. Get away."

"To here?" The touch of incredulity in his voice made her feel small. Whoever escaped to a farmers' market?

"I feel so hemmed in, especially at the shop. We're there all the time. It's all we do."

"No wonder you need a vacation."

"I so do." Now that things had been set in motion, she was going to leave sooner than she had planned, depending on Eloise's reaction.

"Being here has been like a vacation for me. I quite like the slow pace of life. I might stay here a while, buy a nice place near the sea, and spend my time here."

"You're really considering not going back to Boston?"

"I've had a great life in Boston, I've made great contacts and built a business and of course, Maddie grew up there. Susan is still there, but …"

He looked away and she tried to determine if he had regrets. "But I'm now in a different phase of my life, what with the divorce, and Maddie going to college. I'm thinking maybe it's time to make a few changes. How about you?"

She felt strange as he'd been speaking and telling her of his life plans, and yet, it also wasn't that strange that she and Ford were walking around together, talking about their lives as if they did this all the time.

Here was a man who had been her lover over two decades ago. They had each gone their own way and now had come full circle, reconnecting again, and the strangest thing of all was that they weren't talking about trivial things, they were talking about their lives, as if it were normal to do so.

"Ash?"

She glanced up, so deep in her thoughts, she had forgotten to answer him.

"How about you? What are your plans?"

"I feel trapped sometimes," the stark truth tumbled out of her mouth unchecked, and the shocked expression on Ford's face told her that he hadn't been expecting this. "Only sometimes. I mean, not *trapped*, it's not like I'm in a cage or anything, but I feel …" She let out a slow breath as she tried to grapple with her emotions and balance it with what she was telling him. Lulled into a familiar sense of knowing, by the mere action of being by his side, she had to be careful she didn't ramble too much. "I feel …" What was the right word? She didn't want his pity.

"You feel as if you never got a chance to leave and do the things you wanted," he said. Ford not only finished her sentence, he knew her. This was what she had missed. Someone who understood her down to her core. Meeting again after decades apart, they had slipped back into their easygoing and familiar conversation. Being known by someone, like this, like a soulmate would, was priceless. She had never had that level of connection before she'd met him, or since, and now it scared her as much as it excited her.

"That's exactly it."

"And what would you do if you could?"

"I'd run barefoot through the beach and feel the sand between my toes."

"You can do this here. We have the ocean."

"I want somewhere tropical. I want palm trees and coconuts,

pink sand and turquoise blue sea." She did want that, at some point in her life, but what she wanted first was her trip to Europe, and what she didn't want was to tell him that she would soon be making the trip the two of them had planned all that time ago.

Ford stopped walking, they had moved away from the busy market stalls and were at the end of the street with the market spread out in front of them and teeming with people.

"Then you should do that. You should find that beach, and those palm trees with their coconuts, and run barefoot across the sand." He blinked as if it had just occurred to him. "Is that where you're going, somewhere hot and exotic?"

"Uh ..."

"What are you waiting for, Ash?"

"I was waiting for Eloise to get back."

He frowned as if he didn't understand. "I'm sure your sisters can hold down the fort while you're gone. You just have to let them."

"I do have to let go. Ginny thinks I try to control everything, but I can't help it."

"Ginny was too young to remember it all," he said softly.

They exchanged a look that seemed to be caught in a time warp, going back years. She found herself thinking about their first kiss, their first everything. Their dreams and hopes and plans. The images were more vibrant now because he was here, because of his status, and availability, but most of all because no man had ever compared.

He broke the spell first, otherwise she would still have been staring at him. There was no denying the fact. She had missed Ford, and there had been many times when she had hated herself for telling him to go. It had broken her heart when she had learned that he had married, and it was only from that point on, not before, as she'd told him, that she had forced herself to wipe his memory clean off her slate.

"I need to get some vegetables," she said, and they started to walk back towards the stalls, but her mind was elsewhere. She imagined a future that might be different. This time with the possibility that Ford would stay and be a part of it. It was all so early, and pure, and unknown.

This could get tricky, it could go someplace else, become something it had not had a chance before to become.

Her insides fluttered at the idea of a second chance with Ford.

"Maybe we can get together again?" he suggested when they finished shopping and returned to the parking lot, hovering around their cars, ready to return.

"Next time you come here, let me know. It saves us both driving here."

"Better still ..." He pulled out a scrap of paper from his wallet, and a tiny pen, and scribbled down his number and handed it to her. "How about you call me?"

He hadn't asked for her number.

Smart.

He had left it to her to decide if she wanted to meet up again.

She did.

CHAPTER 35

*A*shleigh was in a good mood and making dinner in the kitchen when Eloise and Ginny returned. She asked them how the day had been and specifically wanted to know about a few important matters that had needed to get done. Ginny answered, Eloise said nothing.

Later when they all sat down to eat, Ashleigh was determined to get rid of the stony silence between her and Eloise. Feeling happy from having met Ford earlier, she extended the olive branch first. "I'm sorry I didn't believe you, about being sick all that time. I'm sorry, okay?"

"Someone's in a good mood today," Eloise replied, taking the bowl of roasted potatoes from Ginny, and putting some on her plate.

"I'm sorry."

"And you should be." Eloise passed the bowl to her. "You're always so temperamental, especially when it comes to me."

Ashleigh didn't like the lecture, but was determined to bite her tongue and take the feedback. "It had been a difficult week, and it got the better of me by the time you came home. I've had a good day, and I feel good now. I'm sorry."

Eloise lifted a fork and stabbed a green bean. "Think how much better you'll feel once you go on vacation."

"It's not a vacation. It's not going to be for a few weeks. I'm going for longer."

"Six months," Eloise whined.

She was glad that this was the time frame Eloise had in mind. It would soften the blow. "Two months probably, but it could be as long as four. I'm going to get an open-ended ticket." She hadn't intended to go for that long, but she was testing Eloise, pushing her boundaries and seeing what she could get away with, because if she enjoyed her trip so much, she wanted to have the option to stay longer. She was always going to return. There was no doubt about that.

"Open-ended? What does that mean?" Eloise demanded.

"It means she's never coming back," said Ginny, laughing.

"It could mean that." Ashleigh didn't intend to sound so serious when she said that, but her sisters looked at her as if they believed her.

"You're not coming back?" Ginny cried.

"Of course I'm coming back. What else would I do? Where would I go? I want a break. I'm not leaving you forever."

"Are you going through a mid-life crisis?" Eloise asked. "Why are you doing this?"

"Doing what?" Ashleigh cried, aghast at the push back. She gave Ginny an I-told-you-so look.

Ginny seemed to understand. "Ashleigh deserves a break as much as any of us do."

"Except that it doesn't sound like a break. It sounds like something more permanent. Sounds to me as if you don't want to work here anymore?"

Put on the spot like this, Ashleigh couldn't lie. "I need a few months away. I've never had time away, not quality time, just a week or so here and there, not as much as you—"

"There she goes, blaming us again," Eloise complained. "If you wanted a break, you should have taken it. No one was stopping you."

"Give her a chance to finish," begged Ginny. "Do you feel it's getting harder, working at the shop?" Ginny asked her.

She looked at them both as she weighed her words carefully. "If I'm honest …" If she said what had been playing on her mind, there was a danger that this would be the first domino to fall. Something told her that Eloise was also feeling restless, and was starting to have the same reservations about the business.

She could feel the heat of Eloise's gaze on her. "Don't hold back. Say what you mean," her sister growled.

Ginny put her hand over Ashleigh's. "Do what you feel you need to do, for you. Don't worry about us. We'll be fine."

"What do you mean, don't worry about us? We'll be fine. Who's 'we'? And what exactly are you planning?" Eloise looked at them both as if they'd been plotting something behind her back.

Ginny piped up first. "If you let Ashleigh say her piece, instead of jumping down her throat, she might tell you."

"I'm not jumping down her throat," Eloise retorted. "It feels to me as if the two of you have been scheming something while I've been gone."

"We haven't schemed anything! Ashleigh probably hesitated to say anything in front of you before and judging by your reaction, I can see why—"

Ashleigh looked on in dismay as her sisters started to raise their voices.

"Will you both stop it!" she yelled. "Look at us. Why are we yelling?"

They both looked down at their plates sheepishly. She addressed Eloise first. "I understand you thinking we've been making these plans behind your back. We haven't. I've been thinking of this for months. Months. But it never seemed like the right time." She explained what she had before, that she'd been waiting to tell them of wanting to go away but then Ginny had gotten engaged, and then there was the wedding to plan, and then she was going to tell Eloise after Ginny's bachelorette party, and then all hell broke loose. "It slipped out, when you were away and Ginny and I were talking. She listened, and I told her. And the truth is, where I am now, how I'm feeling, I can't say that I love running the business. I don't even know if I want to be here, in Whisper Falls anymore." Though, lately, with Ford and her talking more, that part of the equation was changing. "I don't want to be running the shop until I'm as old as Aunt Becky was … or even older. I don't want to feel tied down."

"You feel tied down?" Ginny asked, as if this were a revelation.

"Sometimes," Ashleigh replied, noting that Eloise remained silent and didn't even look at them.

"What would you have done if I'd married Ben, and we'd started a family?" Ginny continued. "What if I'd needed some time off? Or maybe not ever come back to work? That won't happen now, because … but, what if I had?"

Ashleigh took a breath, hearing about Ginny's stalled dreams. She and Eloise looked at one another.

She reached for Ginny's hand and squeezed it. "We would have accommodated that." She looked to Eloise for acknowledgement.

"We would have found a way," Eloise answered.

"It's not like that's never going to happen," Ashleigh said softly. "You'll meet someone, one day. Someone worthy of you. You might want to go start that family."

Ginny removed her hand from Ashleigh's. "Let's not talk about the future just yet. I'm still trying to get through the present."

"Honey," Eloise leaned over to Ginny and hugged her. "You

just do what suits you. Don't mind the two of us yelling and screaming at one another. It's when we stop doing that that you'll know something is wrong."

This brought a smile to Ginny's lips.

"Four months?" Eloise asked, her voice losing that hard edge as she picked up her cutlery again.

"At most."

"At most," echoed Eloise pensively, cutting into her chicken. "Four months wouldn't be a stretch. I'm sure we could handle things."

"We can definitely handle things." Ginny agreed.

"Then maybe you should go." Eloise's face had softened. "Just do it. Quit talking about it and just go."

Ginny picked up her glass of water. "That's what I told her."

Ashleigh felt a little flutter of peace float over her. She'd had a good talk with Ford, and now her sisters were happy. And she'd told them she was going. Life was better than it had been in a while.

CHAPTER 36

*E*loise waited until Ginny had gone upstairs. "Has he been over?" she asked Ashleigh, not needing to mention him by name.

"Not since he came to the shop. If he's spoken to Ginny on the phone, she hasn't said."

"She hasn't reacted." This worried Eloise. Ginny had been crazy about Ben. The type of split they'd had warranted more of a response from her sister. Something didn't feel right and she kept thinking that another ugly event loomed on the horizon.

"I hear her crying at night, sometimes. I've gone in and checked on her, but she always says she's okay. We have to give her space. Her friends have been good. She's been seeing them a lot."

They were sitting on the couch in front of the TV. A rom-com was on, something that Eloise hadn't paid much notice to. Given Ginny's situation, they should have looked for something else, more appropriate, but Ginny had claimed that she was tired and gone to bed. Eloise wasn't convinced that her sister was as calm and composed about her situation as she led on.

She and Ashleigh were back to normal, on the surface of

things but Eloise felt some trepidation about her sister's long trip. She'd been so shocked about the length of time away, and by Ashleigh's admission that she sometimes felt tied to the shop, that she hadn't even asked her where she was intending to go. "You should have told me about wanting time off."

"I was going to, after that night at The Connington. But then that whole scenario with Ben happened and I couldn't."

"You've never mentioned being fed up with the business. I thought your life revolved around it."

"My life has revolved around it. I don't have anything else in my life, except the shop. Where dreams begin," she said mockingly. "Not my dreams."

"Maybe now that you're about to embark on your travels, you'll meet someone and your dreams can begin—"

"I don't need a man for my dreams to be fulfilled," Ashleigh shot back. "I'm not traveling in search of a partner."

"You might not be, but you might meet someone. You'll be open to new opportunities," Eloise threw back.

"Is that what you went to Hyannis Port in search of?" Ashleigh asked, her sister's questioning gaze prompting her to suddenly sit upright. Ashleigh sometimes had an uncanny psychic ability to know the real truth from what she was being fed.

"I went for Beth's wedding," she replied in defense. "It was great, being away and with people who like having fun." Darn it. She'd gone and put her foot in it. Again. Ashleigh raised an eyebrow. "That's not what I meant," she backtracked quickly. "Let's not argue. I'm sick of arguing, and if you're leaving us, I don't want to waste time bickering."

"Sounds like a good idea. Can you stick to it?"

"Of course!" She flashed a big wide smile at Ashleigh, because the thought that she might be gone for so many months suddenly sank into her stomach and stayed there, like a brick, heavy and uncomfortable.

Her sister was a glass half-empty type of person. She never used to be. Eloise remembered a time when Ashleigh had been full of fun and daring, and happy, too.

Lately, things had become a bit claustrophobic, with them all working and living together. She sensed that they all wanted their own space. Ginny had almost gotten it. She looked up and examined her sister's face closely, for the first time in a long time, though Ashleigh didn't look too somber tonight.

"I don't have to go right away. I mean, with what happened to Ginny. It doesn't seem fair to lay this on you both."

She already knew from Ginny how Ashleigh had felt and her reluctance to tell Eloise that she wanted to take a break from the business. She was always the more vocal of the sisters, and maybe a little selfish too. It was time she changed things and took a load off Ashleigh's shoulders.

"We've always laid things on you. I'm guilty of doing that a lot, and I'm sorry." She would keep things going. Ashleigh had sacrificed a lot and even if she hadn't taken full advantage of taking long vacations in the past, it was wrong of Eloise to blame her. She could see that her sister had reached a crossroads of some kind. She could feel it in herself, and she had yet to hit her forties. She understood Ashleigh's feeling of wanderlust, because she herself felt it.

"Are you sure?"

"I'm sure." She noticed that there was a warmth in Ashleigh's eyes, and a color in her cheeks.

"Because I can wait, but Ginny says once I'd told you, that there was no point in me hanging around."

"There isn't."

"Will you be okay?"

"You're not going to the moon, Ash. You'll still be on this planet, won't you?" Her sister could be such a drama queen. Such a parent. Of course they were going to be fine. They'd be at each other's throats at times, but they'd be fine.

"I'll be in touch with you constantly."

Eloise picked up a pillow and threw it at her, laughing. "God, no. Please do not be calling me every hour telling me where you are or what you're doing. Where are you going?"

"Europe. Spain, Italy, France, Greece—"

"Is this the trip you and Ford were going to take back in—"

"Not quite."

"Not quite! You were going around Europe. I remember."

"We hadn't planned it in such detail. We were going to go interrailing around Europe." They'd bought passes to visit a multitude of countries by train, traveling light and staying at cheap places.

"And you're going to do that now."

"Except I'm older, and I have taste and more money than I had then. I won't be interrailing, and I've only decided on a few places. I'm going to Spain first, and then I'll plan the next stage of my journey." Ashleigh laughed. "I can't quite believe it."

"That you're going?"

Her sister nodded.

"Are you wearing makeup?" she asked, because Ashleigh was glowing.

Ashleigh touched her face. "No, why?"

"You look really good."

"Thanks."

Her brows pushed together. "Did you get a beauty treatment at The Connington?"

"No!" She pffted, as if this was a ridiculous thing. "I went to the farmers' market." Then she smiled as she lifted a thread from her dress. It wasn't a normal smile either. "I met Ford there."

In that moment, Eloise knew the reason behind her sister's glowing face and happy mood. "That would do it."

"Do what?"

Eloise ignored the question. "You and Ford went to the farmers' market?"

"We didn't go there. I just ran into him there."

Eloise lifted her chin up and appraised Ashleigh's face. "Uh-huh." Her sister tucked her hair behind her ears and shrugged.

"It was no big deal. He was, uh … shopping for vegetables."

"That's what one would hope." She noted that Ashleigh didn't dare to look her in the eye. Before she could question her further, Ashleigh stood up.

"I need to make a list of things that you must take care of. I guess I need to show you the books."

"I can't do the books," Eloise protested.

"No. You can't. We'll figure a way around it. I can do things remotely. You'll have to send me daily figures." She cupped the back of her neck. "There's so much to think about."

Eloise's heart sank at the thought of it. It was all well and good being happy for Ashleigh and her new plans, but her sister had never taken so much time off before, and she was going during the busiest time of the year. Summertime. Four months was an eternity. "Why now?"

"I didn't intend to go now, in the summer. It's just happened that way," Ashleigh reminded her. "If I wait any longer, I'll probably never end up going. That's the story of my life."

"Don't be such a drama queen!" Eloise hurled another pillow at her.

"I'm not!" Ashleigh hurled it back.

"Are we supposed to throw you a going-away party?"

"No. No way. Please don't. Not even a surprise one. I want to walk quietly into the sunset."

"Drama queen."

CHAPTER 37

*A*t least they all knew of her plans to travel. Dropping a hint that running the business until she was in her twilight years wasn't an option she cherished had made Ashleigh felt happier and more at ease. Excitement swirled around her at the idea that she was going to leave and her adventure was about to begin.

All this time she hadn't set a firm date, but in telling her sisters, her plans seemed to have taken on a life of their own. She was leaving in the next two weeks. She had to do it now, before there was any chance of something happening between her and Ford. He still didn't know that it wasn't a short vacation.

Over the next few weeks, they started going to the farmers' market together. She looked for the right moment to tell him, but it hadn't presented itself. They spent their time talking and laughing and catching up on old times, and it didn't seem prudent to mention anything then.

She told Darcie that she'd booked her ticket and hotel for her first destination, but she omitted the news about her and Ford spending more time together. Although this was something that Darcie found out of her own accord when they ran into her one

Sunday at the market. Darcie raised her eyebrow when she saw her and Ford together. Ashleigh would have a lot of explaining to do when they next met.

She was also torn. Spending time with Ford forced her to think about her decision and the length of time she wanted to be away. There were times when she didn't think she was ready to leave.

One day, they were so lost in conversation that they hadn't taken much notice of where they were going. They'd started off at the farmers' market but had veered off to a park nearby.

"A gazebo," Ford announced as they walked towards what looked like an octagonal wooden structure in the middle.

"This is pretty." It was painted white and the top half was open. There were no windows, but it had white poles holding up the slate roof. A wooden railing went all around like a little white picket fence and there were small bushes all around the perimeter.

"Shall we go inside?"

"Sure." Today had been an odd day. They hadn't even pretended to buy vegetables. They hadn't looked at any stalls, except stopping to buy some delicious wraps from a food vendor. They'd sat on a bench near the market, eating and talking and watching the world go by.

She placed her hand on a railing and let the soft breeze caress her face. Ford kept his distance, the way he always did and walked to the end opposite from where she stood.

"It's peaceful, too. I like that. Something you don't get in Boston much." He rested his arm on one of the wooden poles and stared at her, a hint of a smile on his lips.

Even from the distance, she couldn't help but admire his face. Ford was a dream to look at and he had aged so well, it was sinful. Darcie's words circled around her head like screaming vultures.

Some lucky woman will snap him up if you don't.

"I'm going to stay here," he announced.

"In this thing? *Tonight?*"

He laughed, because she had a penchant for saying the most ridiculous things when he was around. "Hardly."

"You mean here, as in Whisper Falls?"

"I feel as if I've come home."

"I don't understand." But she understood enough to know that their conversation had taken a turn for something more serious. For weeks it had been light-hearted fun. He'd never touched her, or accidentally brushed his hand across her skin, even though there had been moments when she'd wished he had.

Her sisters teased her about her frequent visits to the market, and about her spending so much time with Ford, about being away from the shop and doing fun things at weekends. She found herself cocooned in a new closeness that she couldn't describe or label.

What were they? Friends? Acquaintances? Past lovers? Or poised on the precipice of a second chance?

The evening had turned dusky, and it was the longest they had ever spent together. An entire day, starting with breakfast at the diner and ending in this pretty little Gazebo.

"It's something you hear people say all the time, and I finally get what they mean. Coming home doesn't mean just the familiarity of the people and the places I grew up with, or the sounds and smells I'm used to. It's a return to something warm and comforting. Something dependable and solid." He walked towards her, making her feel vulnerable and exposed. She crossed her arms, as if to protect her heart, because the way he looked at her filled her with trepidation and she was suddenly fearful of giving in and changing all her plans.

Thankfully, he stopped an arm's length away from her.

"I love that you're back in my life, Ash."

Her heart sunk. Of all the times he was going to tell her, he'd chosen today.

"Ford ..." She gripped the railing with both hands, looking far into the distance because she didn't want to see the hope in his eyes get crushed. "Don't."

He didn't listen. "I've missed you, and even though it was wrong, because we were still married, there were times, in the two years that Susan and I separated, that I found myself thinking of you."

"Don't."

"Let me say what I need to. I'm not asking for anything. I just need you to know."

She faced him, giving in, prepared to listen. "I gave my all to my wife for the entire time we were married. There truly was no one else, but after we separated, I would be lying if I said I didn't think of you. You're always on my mind, Ash, and I can't help thinking of you. If you want to know the truth of it, I fall in love with you a little more each time I see you."

Her mouth fell open at his admission and her heart softened to mush. "Oh, Ford." It had been a feat of endurance to remain strong and disciplined spending time with him by her side. He'd been such a gentleman, never making a move or an inappropriate gesture that at times she had wondered if her attraction to him was one- sided.

At least now she knew.

He looked at her with eyes so shiny and clear, so full of hope that, for a moment, she considered ditching her dreams. She could so easily forget Europe and stay here to see how she and Ford ended up. After all these years, they had another chance at life and love.

But she was on a different journey. *Her* journey, to do with *her* dreams. It didn't mean that she didn't feel the same way about him—if she left. It only meant that for once she was putting herself first.

"Uh …" he said slowly, looking deflated. "You don't feel the same way."

"I do." She swallowed, clearing her throat as she allowed the truth to unfurl. She wanted to remember this moment, the way he looked at her, and how it would all change. Being bold, she lifted her hand to his face, the cells in her body tingling as memories flooded back. It wasn't so soft anymore, his skin, not the way she remembered it, but tougher, slightly leathery, not as smooth. "I do feel the same way. I love that you're back in my life. I love the time we've spent together. I've been more alive in these past weeks with you than I have in the past few years."

"You have?" His voice was laced thick with incredulity, a testament to how good a job she'd done holding herself in check around him.

She nodded. He placed his hand over hers, then moved it away from his face. "So, me moving back here might work for both of us … maybe? If we take it slow. I don't want you to feel pressured. I like it here, and you being here makes everything perfect."

She cleared her throat. "That vacation I told you about?"

His brow furrowed as if he couldn't understand what that had to do with anything.

"It's not a two-week vacation." She extricated her hand from his.

"No?" He smiled goofily, but she didn't smile back, wanting to prepare him for the news she was sure he wouldn't like.

"I'm going away for a few months—"

"A few months? Why so long?"

"I've been stuck here my whole life and I want to fly."

He tilted his head as if he didn't understand.

"I want to do what we couldn't do back then, when my parents …"

There was an understanding in his eyes. "You want to get away. Escape to somewhere where there are palm trees and coconuts."

"I don't know why I said that." Coconuts had become fixated in her brain, and she blamed Eloise's duffel for that. Her travel destinations didn't have palm trees and coconuts. "I'm going to Europe."

"You're traveling around Europe, Ash?" In that quiet and unspoken moment, she knew instinctively what he was thinking.

That she was going without him.

"Not interrailing. I'm too old for that." She could see that this had come as a huge shock to him. "Something more comfortable. Luxury hotels and flights. No trains, if I can help it."

"Europe doesn't have palm trees and coconuts," he pointed out.

"That will be my next trip. For now, I want coffee and croissants in Paris, and palmiers in Venice."

"Palmiers are French." He surveyed her face carefully, as if he were trying to decode her thoughts to figure out her reasoning. Why Europe? Why now? That's what he probably wanted to know.

"Since when did you become such a food connoisseur? I've seen pictures of a shop in Venice that sells the most delectable-looking pastries. That's where I want to go."

"Why the need to escape?" His voice, husky and low, was almost a whisper.

"You got to go away and do things, things you had planned for—"

"I was ready to come back for you, I would have stayed here."

"This isn't about that, Ford. I didn't want to ruin your dreams."

"Who says my dreams would have been ruined if I'd stayed here? Maybe this feels like home because this was where I was meant to be all along."

"In this gazebo?" She tried to inject some humor into a conversation she feared was going to turn too heavy too fast.

"With you."

She held her breath, wondering what to say, whether to encourage him or to put a stop to that type of thinking. "We'll never know because we only get one shot at life. I don't regret staying here to take care of my family, but now ..." She paused and looked away. "Now I'm ready to explore and see what I've been missing. I want to make my dreams come true. I want to do something for me."

He was silent for a while, then, "How long for?"

"Two months, maybe three, maybe four."

"Why so long?"

"I have this yearning to be out there in the world. I feel stuck. I've been wanting to go away for a while, but I stayed for Ginny, for the wedding. I've been in Whisper Falls all my life, Ford. I never got a chance to get away. My wings were clipped."

"Ash." His eyes sought hers and she feared for what he might say, what he might ask of her, even though he had no right to ask anything.

"I'm doing this for me. I have to. Please let me."

His Adam's apple moved, and she could see that he was holding up pretty well, but the light had gone out of his eyes. He gave a laugh, but it was half-hearted, as if he wanted to show her that he was happy for her but couldn't bring himself to feel it. "You're coming back, though, aren't you?"

"Of course. Yes, of course I'm coming back. Where do you think I'm going to go?"

His face turned somber and he gazed at the ground as he reached for her hand again. He was processing things, and this news needed to sink in and settle. She'd hit him with it, and judging by his reaction, he hadn't expected this at all.

It would have been so easy to make the decision to stay, but she would have regretted it forever. It was so simple and seductive, spending her free time with Ford, getting to know one another again, enjoying meals and walks, and remembering the past with a cautious glimpse towards the future, but she didn't want to get too cosy with him because then she ran the risk of falling head over heels with him all over again, headfirst and hard, and then she would never leave.

It was difficult enough already.

"I've planned my trip out, and I can extend my stay wherever I go. If I want to stay for longer in Amalfi, I can, and I will."

"The Amalfi Coast?" he asked softly.

"I've always wanted to go there."

"It was the—"

"I know." The Amalfi Coast had been the final place where they were supposed to end up and splurge out in the final part of their trip.

The silence between them twisted and twined uncomfortably. She prayed that he wouldn't ask if he could come along, somehow suggesting that they now take the trip they had canceled all those years ago.

This wasn't about her needing more time with Ford in order to relive that past. This was about her claiming her stake in the future she had envisioned for herself and not letting anything, or anyone, derail it.

If she stayed, just because Ford wasn't returning to Boston, if she stayed because of him, because it felt right and good and it made sense, she would be doing a disservice to herself and her dreams. She would be doing what she always did; the right thing, the safe thing. While it made perfect sense to be here with this man whom she was starting to have feelings for, she owed it to herself to be footloose and fancy-free, because if she didn't do that now, then when would she ever?

Her desire to leave, to travel, not just physically, but in the mind, to do new things, to become a new her, was strong, and if she asked Ford to come along with her, she would be comprising everything.

"I want you to have the most amazing trip of your life, and I applaud that you're doing this, chasing a dream you've had. You deserve it, Ash. I'll be waiting for you when you come back, unless you tell me to stop waiting."

She couldn't stop the smile from spreading on her face. A dizzying sensation swirled in the base of her belly. Ford's eyes were full of hope, shining and happy. The smile on his lips had spread all the way up.

They faced one another, holding hands.

"That's the thing with you and me," she said. "We always have bad timing." Just then, the fairy lights on the gazebo came on. She gasped in delight.

"I'd say that was great timing." His thumb slid over her fingers, caressing gently. How easy it would be to stay here, to forget about her trip, and see how things developed between her and Ford. She was starting to look forward to their dinners, and lunches, and their walks, their visits to the farmers' market and the park. She was beginning to enjoy his company, her heart rate speeding up each time she got ready to meet him.

She could give it all up and stay here, but it would be the wrong decision.

Even Ford knew that.

"If you meet a tall, dark and handsome Italian or Spaniard, I'll step aside."

She laughed. "I'm going to find out about myself. I don't want to get involved with someone. This is a journey for me."

"I know."

She remembered something. "Did you … did you used to talk to my sisters? Whenever you came back, when you were married, I mean?"

"All the time. Why?" He frowned as if she were asking something odd. "Am I not allowed to talk to them?"

It was true, then. "But we hardly ever talked."

"It doesn't mean I didn't want to know how you were. Life hit you with the biggest curveball, Ash. I couldn't just forget about you. I had to know that things were working out. Why are you asking?"

She lifted each shoulder slowly, easing out the tightness that was buried into her muscles from hunching over her computer. "It was a shock to me, to see you and Ginny talking as if you'd known one another your whole lives."

"I have known her all her life. She was so tiny back then. Eloise would always talk to me if she saw me."

"That little minx. She never said a word." If there was a diploma in secrecy, Eloise would have a dozen of them.

"She probably knew you'd tell her to stop talking to me if you'd found out."

"Eloise takes no notice of what I say," Ashleigh quipped with a smile.

"It's pretty late," he said, looking out. The sky was dappled pink and purple. "We should go." He touched her face, then thumbed her lower lip. Their gazes locked and held, caught in a timeless moment. She wanted him to kiss her, and when his gaze fell to her lips, she felt herself turn giddy, waiting for the heady moment when his lips would press against hers and send her back in time, when he used to kiss and make her toes curl, hold her as if he would never let go. It was all coming back to her now, caught up in this electric bubble that encased them both. She almost closed her eyes, expecting to feel his lips on hers and his hand around her waist, but instead he kissed his forefinger and touched her lips.

"I'll still be here … whenever you decide to come back, Ash." His gaze locked with hers, his voice was so low it whispered inside her, speaking directly to her heart.

This was it? This was their goodbye?

"I will come back." There was no question about it. She would return. Nothing could keep her away now.

"Will you?" He raised a finger to her cheek and stroked it. Her skin warmed to his touch. With his blue eyes locking onto hers, a battle of wills seemed to be brewing inside her. Her heart begged her to stay, pleading for this second chance at love as it clashed with her brain, where logic and reasoning told her she had to leave.

To stick to her plans.

"I have something to come back for now, I think."

"You think?" Blue eyes shone under the fairy lights, and when his hand slipped around her neck, her heart almost jumped out. A move so bold, it surprised her.

But it was nothing compared to when he kissed her.

It was a light press first. He seemed to be testing, sensing, gauging her response. When the press of his hands around her waist sent tingles all over her body, it wasn't butterflies that skimmed around inside her, but a riot of emotions which ripped through her. Her lips parted, welcoming him and when their kiss deepened, she fell into him, their bodies touching lightly at first, a homecoming, of sorts.

Pain and pleasure, regret and relief, goodbye and hello, all rolled into one all-consuming emotion. She slid her arms around his neck, pressing closer.

It wasn't until now that she understood just how much she'd missed him.

So much.

She'd regretted letting him go, and had buried this feeling deep inside her, but now he was helping it all to shake loose.

Her hands slipped down to his shoulders, and in that moment, with their mouths still joined, she felt the difference. Broad, wide and thick; the shoulders of a man, not the boy she had turned away.

They kissed again, making up for lost time. Tasting him, and feeling his skin and the hardness of his body against hers, made her moan. Joy danced in every cell of her body. He tilted his head back and stared down at her with a tenderness that was both old and new. They had been young adults when he'd last looked at her like that, kissed her and held her like that, when the world had been theirs for the taking.

"Ash," he murmured, pulling her closer. "*My* Ash."

She blinked, frozen in shock because it was all coming back.

My Ash.

He used to call her that. How had she forgotten? How had she completely erased it from her mind?

She buried her face in his chest, inhaling the strong manly pine-and-mint scent of him. To hug him was to feel safe and protected, to no longer feel alone, but to belong.

To have someone.

Someone she had loved deeply once upon a time, then let go, until life and circumstance had brought them back together.

"Oh, Ford." She tip-toed up, and met his mouth, their lips joining again as he kissed her with more fervor this time. It was a kiss of remembering, of yearning, of a lost past, and the promise of a better future.

She loved him.

It was engrained deep within her bones, a truth which now floated to the surface.

She pulled away, and they stared into each other's eyes. No

words, no smiles, but a deep connectedness binding them together. She knew, could feel what he was thinking.

"I love you. I don't think I ever really stopped." His words floated around her like a feather, stroking her gently and reeling her into this beautiful new dream.

CHAPTER 38

"*P*assport," Ginny said.

Ashleigh's eyes locked on it. It was lying on her bedside cabinet. "Check."

"Laptop."

"Check."

"Charger cables."

"Check."

Ginny continued to read down the list that Ashleigh had prepared, and ticked off everything, again. Ashleigh was paranoid about leaving something behind.

"Cell phone battery pack and chargers."

"Check." The battery pack was for when she was out and about. The chargers were for the hotel room. "Cell phone, add cell phone to the list!"

"You won't forget your cell phone," Ginny said quietly.

"Add it to the—"

"All right. Calm down. I will." Ginny scribbled it down. "You're not going to forget your cell phone, trust me."

This was the final check. Everything had been packed, and her clothes for tomorrow were laid out on her chair.

Eloise was cooking dinner. It would be an early dinner, Ashleigh had decided, because she wanted to go see Darcie for one last time.

"I think that's everything." Ginny handed her the sheet of paper. Ashleigh glanced at it then surveyed the chaos of clothes and documents lying on her bed. She had taken a few clothes out of her suitcase, preferring to travel as lightly as possible.

"I can't believe you're finally going." Ginny beamed at with pride.

"No need to look so happy. I can't believe I'm going myself." The smell of tacos wafted through the air. "Do you want to go through the business book one last time?"

"No."

"But—"

"No."

She wished Ginny would stop being so laidback about everything. Her sisters teased her and the many lists she had made; lists for herself, like the one Ginny had checked items off on, and the list of the million and one things to keep on top of for the business. The so-called business book was a master list of items Ashleigh had put together for her sisters to refer to. A systems and procedures manual which contained anything and everything to do with the shop. All the orders that Ashleigh was aware of; dresses that were due to be collected and couriered over to brides-to-be, as well as daily, weekly and monthly business matters that needed to be taken care of. She felt uneasy that Ginny didn't want to go through it for one last time.

"Tacos are ready!" Eloise shouted.

Ginny made a face, wrinkling her nose. Ashleigh frowned. "You love tacos."

"Not the way Eloise makes them."

"I'm starving. Let's eat."

They sat around the table, having dinner for one last time.

Ashleigh wondered how things would be, and what would have changed by the time she got back.

"Drink up," Eloise ordered, refilling her half-empty wine glass.

"I'm going over to Darcie's after, and she's threatened me with more wine."

"You've hardly touched yours," Eloise exclaimed, looking at Ginny's full glass and her barely touched taco.

"I'm not hungry."

"I'm going to miss these," Ashleigh announced.

Eloise got ready to take a bite from the side of her taco. "I'm sure they do tacos where you're going. They're a universal food item. Like water."

"I'm not so sure." Ashleigh reached for another one. Here she was on the eve of her departure, eating tacos and tomorrow she would be gone. Her eyes welled up as a profound sense of sadness came over her. She'd been looking forward to her 'great escape' for months, but now that it was here, she felt inexplicably somber. And empty. Or was it numbness? "I'll call every day."

"Please don't," begged Ginny.

"Oh, no. No, you won't," Eloise told her, both of them speaking at almost the same time.

"How about every other day?" Ashleigh suggested.

Eloise licked her lips and got ready to take another bite. "Do you want us to concentrate on the business?"

"Or do you want us to waste time telling you about every little minute detail?" asked Ginny. "Because that's what you'll be doing. You'll want to know every little thing that took place every single day."

Ashleigh felt a little bruised at the thought that her sisters didn't want to hear from her.

"You could call Ford instead and speak to him," Eloise suggested, an evil glint in her eye.

Ginny chimed in. "She *is* going to call him every day."

"You should have asked him to come over for tacos."

Before she could open her mouth to say anything, Ginny piped up. "She had breakfast with him this morning. This is her having quality time with her sisters now."

"Is that what they call it?" Eloise lifted her glass as the two of them continued to talk about her as if she wasn't there.

"Seeing that we've barely had much time with her of late, we should be grateful for this sliver of time that Ashleigh's giving us," Ginny commented.

"Yes, we should." Eloise and Ginny clinked their glasses together.

"All right. That's enough. I would have invited Ford tonight, but I wanted to have our last meal with just us." The lump in her throat mushroomed as she lifted her wine glass. Her hand shook. She forced herself to be strong, not wanting to fall apart on this of all evenings. Her sisters didn't appear to be sad about her going. So why was she?

"To the next four months, to health and happiness, to good times and togetherness."

"As together as it's possible to be with four thousand miles of the Atlantic between us," said Eloise dryly, as she clinked her glass.

"Togetherness." Ginny clinked hers before setting it down. She reached for Ashleigh's hand. "We have Zoom and so many other ways of keeping in touch. We won't notice the distance. It will be as if you're still here with us."

Ashleigh squeezed her hand, appreciating Ginny's words.

"I can't lie though," Ginny continued. "I'm going to really miss you." Her eyes filled up instantly. The hard exterior she had put up seemed to be dismantling before their eyes. All of the pain which Ben had put her through, the pain she had not acknowledged fully, seemed to be seeping out now. Ashleigh still worried about her.

"I'm going to be fine," Ginny assured her. As if to prove a point, she took a deep breath in and composed herself.

"Of course she'll be fine," Eloise said. "I'll be taking care of her."

Ashleigh and Ginny burst out laughing.

"What? What did I say that was so funny?"

They met in Darcie's backyard, with a bottle of Chardonnay on the table before them, and two half-full glasses.

Now that she finally had a moment to tell her, Ashleigh recounted the encounter with Ford last week. "He said he'd be waiting for me when I come back, or until I tell him not to."

"Oh, hon." Darcie got out of her chair, came up behind her and put her arms around her neck. "I think he's in love with you, hon."

"He said he's always loved me."

"What?" Darcie came around and sat back in her chair, sitting forward eagerly, her elbows on her knees, her eyes wide like a child's. "He said that?"

Ashleigh nodded.

"That man is such a romantic. Why didn't you tell me sooner?"

"I'm telling you now. It's been crazy for me lately, trying to get my travel and the business figured out."

"But this is big news. *Huge*." Darcie slapped her on the knee lightly. "I can't believe you didn't tell me."

"I'm falling in love with him all over again."

"I love this. I freaking love this!" Darcie shrieked. "I don't know why you're crying. It's the best news."

Ashleigh dabbed at her eyes, confused by her reaction and the whirlwind of emotions which swirled through her. She had a chance to be with the man she had truly loved, a man who was available, and a man who would be waiting for her when she returned to Whisper Falls.

She felt complete; happier than she had in a long time. Not only was she going off on her own little adventure, she was doing so secure in the knowledge that her sisters would be fine but more so that they had given her their blessing.

Their blessing.

She lowered her head. To someone else, it might have sounded archaic, but she couldn't have gone knowing that Eloise had a problem with it. While Ginny had been her biggest champion, it was Eloise's approval she had needed. Something in her sister had changed recently. She seemed calmer, and more laidback.

As for Ginny, Ashleigh worried about leaving her so soon, especially since Ginny hadn't been eating well lately. She'd been tired and nauseous and Ashleigh worried that the real stress of what had happened with Ben was only just manifesting.

She also wanted to stay around for another month in case that weasel tried to sneak back in and entice Ginny, but Ginny was adamant for her to be gone. Every single day, she told Ashleigh that she was fine.

Now, sitting here with Darcie, Ashleigh gazed up at the pink-splattered sky with its gold and blue hues. In a few days' time she would stare at this same sky but from Barcelona.

She would return to Whisper Falls, of course she would. She had good reason for it. Not obligation, or duty, for her sisters were all grown up now and had lives of their own. She needed to remember that.

Ford's blue eyes suddenly appeared in her mind's eye, and her lips curved into a smile, remembering his smile. Her insides jiggled with joy. She had something to come back here for. A fun and exciting new reason.

But before that, she had an adventure to set off on. New people, new places, new experiences. The world beckoned, and she, Ashleigh Rose, was ready to meet it head on.

Thank you for reading THE BRIDAL SHOP! I hope you enjoyed reading Ashleigh's story. Find out what happens to Ashleigh and her sisters in the follow-up books. Eloise's story will be next.

SIGN UP FOR MY NEWSLETTER to find out when new books release:
https://www.siennacarr.com/newsletter

I appreciate your help in spreading the word, including telling a friend, and I would be grateful if you could leave a review on your favorite book site.

Thank you so much!
Sienna

ACKNOWLEDGMENTS

I would like to thank my amazing group of proofreaders who check my manuscript for errors, typos and inconsistencies.

I am eternally grateful for their help and support:

Marcia Chamberlain
Dena Pugh
Carole Tunstall

I would also like to thank Tatiana Vila of Vila Design for creating this awesome cover.

ABOUT THE AUTHOR

Sienna Carr has been writing romance since 2013. She lives in the UK with her husband, three children, and a parrot.

Connect with Me

I love hearing from you – so please don't be shy!
You can email me at: sienna@siennacarr.com

Find me on :
BookBub
Goodreads
Website - https://www.siennacarr.com

Printed in Great Britain
by Amazon

68380714R00137